SEARCH FOR A WIFE

After dinner they went into the blue drawing room where coffee and liqueurs were waiting for them and the Marquis had hardly had a sip of his before his aunt said,

"I am going to leave you two young people to get to know each other. I hope, Ivor, you will listen to what Edith has to say and I am sure you will find it interesting."

She did not wait for the Marquis to reply because she suspected he might protest and slipped out of the room closing the door firmly behind her.

He went to stand in front of the fireplace wondering what he should say and how he could avoid what he felt could be an uncomfortable *tête-á-tête*.

Then to his surprise Edith looked up at him and said in a small rather frightened voice,

"I am sorry! So very sorry!"

The Marquis looked down at her and thought if he was honest she was not completely unattractive – she was just young, unfledged and dull.

Then because of what she had said, he replied,

"I am afraid my aunt is very tactless and like all my family, she cannot help matchmaking without concerning herself with my feelings."

"You don't really want to – marry me?" she asked, stumbling over her words.

The Marquis shook his head.

"Quite frankly, no! I have no wish at the moment to marry anyone."

THE BARBARA CARTLAND
PINK COLLECTION

Titles in this series

SEARCH FOR A WIFE

BARBARA CARTLAND

Barbaracartland.com Ltd

THE BARBARA CARTLAND PINK COLLECTION

Dame Barbara Cartland is still regarded as the most prolific bestselling author in the history of the world.

In her lifetime she was frequently in the Guinness Book of Records for writing more books than any other living author.

Her most amazing literary feat was to double her output from 10 books a year to over 20 books a year when she was 77 to meet the huge demand.

She went on writing continuously at this rate for 20 years and wrote her very last book at the age of 97, thus completing an incredible 400 books between the ages of 77 and 97.

Her publishers finally could not keep up with this phenomenal output, so at her death in 2000 she left behind an amazing 160 unpublished manuscripts, something that no other author has ever achieved.

Barbara's son, Ian McCorquodale, together with his daughter Iona, felt that it was their sacred duty to publish all these titles for Barbara's millions of admirers all over the world who so love her wonderful romances.

So in 2004 they started publishing the 160 brand new Barbara Cartlands as *The Barbara Cartland Pink Collection*, as Barbara's favourite colour was always pink – and yet more pink!

The Barbara Cartland Pink Collection is published monthly exclusively by Barbaracartland.com and the books are numbered in sequence from 1 to 160.

Enjoy receiving a brand new Barbara Cartland book each month by taking out an annual subscription to the Pink Collection, or purchase the books individually.

The Pink Collection is available from the Barbara Cartland website www.barbaracartland.com via mail order and through all good bookshops.

In addition Ian and Iona are proud to announce that The Barbara Cartland Pink Collection is now available in ebook format as from Valentine's Day 2011.

For more information, please contact us at:

Barbaracartland.com Ltd.
Camfield Place
Hatfield
Hertfordshire AL9 6JE
United Kingdom

Telephone: +44 (0)1707 642629
Fax: +44 (0)1707 663041
Email: info@barbaracartland.com

THE LATE DAME BARBARA CARTLAND

Barbara Cartland who sadly died in May 2000 at the age of nearly 99 was the world's most famous romantic novelist who wrote 723 books in her lifetime with worldwide sales of over 1 billion copies and her books were translated into 36 different languages.

As well as romantic novels, she wrote historical biographies, 6 autobiographies, theatrical plays, books of advice on life, love, vitamins and cookery. She also found time to be a political speaker and television and radio personality.

She wrote her first book at the age of 21 and this was called *Jigsaw*. It became an immediate bestseller and sold 100,000 copies in hardback and was translated into 6 different languages. She wrote continuously throughout her life, writing bestsellers for an astonishing 76 years. Her books have always been immensely popular in the United States, where in 1976 her current books were at numbers 1 & 2 in the B. Dalton bestsellers list, a feat never achieved before or since by any author.

Barbara Cartland became a legend in her own lifetime and will be best remembered for her wonderful romantic novels, so loved by her millions of readers throughout the world.

Her books will always be treasured for their moral message, her pure and innocent heroines, her good looking and dashing heroes and above all her belief that the power of love is more important than anything else in everyone's life.

" 'Love me forever' may be the title of a popular song and in my books the hero and the heroine always fall in love for ever and remain faithful to each other throughout Eternity, but in the world we live in today for ever does seem an impossible dream, but to romantics like me and most of my readers love does last for ever and always will."

Barbara Cartland

CHAPTER ONE
1816

The Marquis of Milverton alighted from his very up-to-date high phaeton and walked into White's Club, a place he knew he could always meet his friends.

At this moment he needed them badly.

White's Club in St. James's Street was undoubtedly the most prestigious Club in London. Its many rules of membership were extremely strict and every member was obliged to agree to obey all of them.

Anyone who was turned down by White's kept it, if possible, a dark secret as they felt ashamed that they would not shine with the other bucks who had become of great Social significance during the reign of the Prince Regent.

Among the many illustrious Regency personalities who were members of White's, the Prince Regent himself was the most remarkable.

The Marquis had been a member since his father had proposed him when he was old enough – and his uncle and grandfather had been members too.

To him, like a great number of his friends, it was a second home to which they went inevitably once or twice a day when they were resident in London.

On entering the Club the Marquis nodded to the porters who chorused,

"Good morning, my Lord."

1

He then made his way into the smoking room and, as he expected, three of his friends were there already and he expected more would turn up later.

Harry, the Earl of Landock jumped up to greet him.

"I thought you would be here this morning, Ivor," he began. "I am very anxious to know if you are running your horse in the race at Epsom tomorrow."

"Of course I will be running him, Harry."

The Marquis sat down next to the Earl and another of his good friends, Lord Dromont, and ordered a glass of champagne.

"You are starting early, Ivor," observed the Earl.

"I need it," he answered, "after what I went through last night."

Two other friends who had followed the Marquis into the room sat down near Lord Dromont and asked,

"What has happened, Ivor?"

"I will tell you later. Just now I need sustenance and nothing is better for that condition than champagne!"

"We all agree with you there," they chortled.

A Steward arrived with a large bottle of champagne and started pouring it out and as he was doing so two other elegant young gentlemen joined them.

"We missed you while you were away, Ivor," one greeted him. "We are longing to hear what happened."

"I thought you would be," replied the Marquis.

He told his friends before he left for the country to join his family that his uncle was producing an attractive young girl for him.

In addition, he was told, she was an heiress and his uncle thought she would make him an excellent wife.

"What was she like?" the Earl asked breathlessly as the Steward, having filled up their glasses, walked away.

"Ghastly!" the Marquis answered.

The word made his group of friends look at him in astonishment.

"Ghastly?" one of them questioned. "But you were told she was a beauty, charming and immensely rich."

"That was the only attribute that was true about her. She was plain, extremely stupid and I can never imagine a worse *hell* than being married to her!"

"So what did you do about it?"

"I ran away as soon as I could! I have decided I will never stay with my family again until they promise to stop pushing me into matrimony. In point of fact I cannot stand any more of it!"

"Do you think they will listen to you?"

There was a pause before the Marquis responded,

"I would certainly doubt it, but I have no intention of marrying anyone simply because my uncle and the rest of my tiresome relations have chosen her for me. If I do marry – and at the moment it is very doubtful – it will be to someone I really want as my wife."

There was a murmur and then the Earl said,

"That is just what we all want, Ivor, but you know as well as I do that because we are who we are, we will continue to be pestered, pleaded with and if at all possible *trapped* into matrimony."

"That is true," chipped in Lord Dromont, who had not previously spoken.

He was a good-looking young man of twenty-six, noted for his vast estate in the Midlands as well as a Castle in Scotland – he had been labelled as 'an important catch' ever since he came to London.

It was only by sheer dexterity that he had managed not to be pushed up the aisle by his determined relatives or to be caught by ambitious mothers of *debutantes*.

In fact all the young gentlemen round the Marquis were, as they began to tell him now, continually pleaded with or bullied by their relatives.

"If I ever hear anyone say again, 'but you have to provide an heir', I think I will run away from London and go round the world!" one young Lord exclaimed.

"If you think you have suffered from your relatives, you should try mine," another piped up. "They talk about some girl until I am sick of hearing her name before I have even met her, then when I do see her she is inevitably very different from all they have told me about her."

There was laughter and another added,

"You should see the horror produced for me a week ago. She was incredibly fat and incapable of carrying on a conversation about anything except herself. My father was certain I should be happy with her especially as she would have a dowry almost as big as she was herself!"

"That, of course, was the attraction," another Lord declared sarcastically.

"Then you will all have to be like me," the Marquis told them, "and refuse to go home at all if there is a woman waiting to pounce on one the moment one arrives."

The Earl laughed.

"That of course depends on the woman. Enough women have pounced on you, Ivor, to make you cynical when you meet some unfledged chit who has only just left the schoolroom."

"That is true, Harry. At the same time how can one be certain they will turn into the attractive, witty married ladies with whom we all spend so much of our time?"

"It would certainly be very silly to spend more than ten minutes with a *debutante*. You would be told you had ruined her reputation and the only way to escape the wrath and fury of her father was to offer her a wedding ring."

"That is true enough," another voice came in. "We agree with Ivor, we will just have to stay away from home until they stop imploring us to marry some idiotic girl one would be bored stiff with before one reached the Church!"

There was silence before another comment,

"The trouble is I like going home. I am very fond of my mother and we have the best horses in Kent."

"As you cannot marry a horse, old boy, you will have to marry the untrained fledgling chosen for you!"

There was laughter, but the sad expressions on their faces told the Marquis all too clearly they were suffering the way he was.

Because they had all been at Eton they were all much the same age, some were twenty-five, others like him were twenty-six or nearing twenty-seven.

All his friends who had married when they were younger were mostly living in the country and only visited London on special occasions.

When they did so they came to White's and wanted to hear all the gossip they had missed and yet the Marquis had often thought they seemed to have become duller and less amusing than they had been before they married.

He looked round quizzically at his friends.

While they had been talking two others had joined them making the party up to seven and he thought they were as lucky as he to have remained single for so long.

The Steward was already filling up the glasses from another bottle when the Marquis raised his hand.

"I am going to propose a toast to bachelorhood and may all of us remain unwed for at least another three or four years!"

"I'll drink to that," the Earl agreed eagerly.

Then as they all raised their glasses, Lord Dromont spoke for the second time,

"It is all very well for us to feel so optimistic about this, but we have to face facts and sooner or later we will have to be married whether we like it or not."

He put up his hand to stop any protests and added,

"It is simply because our titles and our possessions which have all been in the family for generations must be preserved. Like Ivor I am an only son. Even though I hate my relations fussing me, I know that they are right. I must produce an heir to make certain of the inheritance."

For a moment all their faces were serious and then they realised that however much they might rebel they had a responsibility which was undeniable – and it was one to which, sooner or later, they would have to conform.

"What I want to know," one friend asked, "is why the young women today are so unattractive? We have all lost our hearts at one time or another to the attractive ladies who must remain nameless inside this Club because they are married. Then why are the new generation of young girls so incredibly boring and to put it bluntly – *plain*?"

Listening to him the Marquis realised that his friend was saying something he had often thought himself, but he had, however, found no answer to this question.

Debutantes were paraded in front of him like horses at a Spring Sale and they had been not only unattractive but boring. When he had danced with them, they had been incapable of carrying on a conversation about anything of interest. They giggled, blushed and made no response if he was witty and even less if he was serious.

It was all very well, he told himself, for his family to say they would grow into the delightful charming ladies he spent a great deal of his time with.

But how could he be certain he would be so lucky? He might be tied to an incredible bore for the rest of his life!

"I know exactly what you are thinking, Ivor," the Earl remarked, "I have often thought the same. But surely there must be girls somewhere who are really attractive?

"They would entice us in the same way as we are enticed by those gorgeous creatures who wait until their husbands are called to the country or busy in Parliament before they give us all we ask of them."

This was plain speaking and the Earl looked up to a murmur of agreement like a roll of thunder.

"You are quite right, Harry. If one thinks it out, there must be girls somewhere we could really fall in love with."

"Indeed there must be," Lord Dromont thundered. "The point is that here in London we do not meet them. To put it plainly we should have to seek them out rather than have them fall into our arms like overripe peaches."

The Marquis laughed.

"Of course you are right, Tony, but the question is – and it's quite simple – where do we look?"

"Anywhere except in London. If you ask me the last one any of us really want to marry is one of the Social girls whose whole ambition is to be asked to Carlton House and who has been brought up to believe heaven on earth exists only in a ballroom!"

The other men stared at him.

"You have a point there," one said. "My sister was married before her Season to a man who lived locally and who she fell in love with. And I have never seen a happier couple who live only for each other."

Another voice came in,

"You are right. There was a girl who I met in the country and I thought seriously of asking her to marry me. But I was too slow, so my best friend stepped in in front of me and now they have two children and are the happiest couple I know."

"What you are saying is that we are looking in the wrong place. We are all expecting to find Aphrodite the Goddess of Love in Carlton House! If she was there, His Royal Highness would have surely stepped in front of us!"

There was a burst of laughter.

If you ask me, Tony is right and we are looking in the wrong place. We are just not going to find someone beautiful, intelligent and so different in a London drawing oom and certainly not amongst the Cyprians we all find entrancing for an odd evening or two."

"Well then, where do you suggest we look?" Lord Dromont enquired.

"I think the answer is anywhere except where we are at this very moment," the Marquis replied. "But only of course if you are serious in thinking that to have an heir you have to take a wife."

He knew only too well as the only son the title of his family he was so proud of would have to be carried on.

There was also a great house and a great estate that had belonged to the Milvertons for hundreds of years and each generation spent money on it and made it even finer.

However much they might say they found married ladies desirable, each and every one of them sitting round him at this moment knew where their duty lay.

They all had eventually to find a wife and create a home where their children could be brought up.

The Steward came up with a new bottle and as he filled up their glasses an elderly gentleman in the corner of the Club rose to his feet.

As he approached, the Marquis realised it was the Duke of Sandelford who had been a friend of his father and had known him since he was a small boy.

"You must forgive me, Ivor," began the Duke, "if I have been listening to your conversation and I admit that I found it extremely interesting."

"I am sorry if we disturbed you, Your Grace."

"It did not disturb me particularly, my boy, except that I thought you had discussed with candour a question that arises in every generation and has been the subject of concern to the older members of every historic family since the beginning of time."

The Marquis laughed.

"I thought you would appreciate our difficulties, Your Grace."

"I not only appreciate them, but I am sympathetic, which you may find difficult to understand because I am so much older. But it was an issue that worried me in exactly the same way when I was your age."

The young gentlemen were listening intently now as the Duke continued,

"I solved my problem and was fortunate enough to marry a woman who I loved dearly and who loved me. I am proud to say she is still my wife.

"As Ivor will know I was fortunate enough to have three sons. One of them was in the Army and was killed in action. Another of my sons suffers from ill health – he is certainly not strong enough to be married. I am therefore dependent on my third son who I am thankful to say after producing two daughters has at last given me a grandson."

9

"Congratulations Your Grace," they chorused.

"I am naturally very happy, but what you have said is so true that to find a woman who will make *you* happy for the rest of your life is exceedingly difficult."

He paused and looked round before he added,

"I, as I have already told you, have been very lucky. But many of my friends have endured years of misery and indifference simply because they were forced into marriage by their families and did not really love with their hearts and souls the woman they had taken as a wife."

He was speaking slowly, but they were all listening.

"What I am going to suggest to you now is that you must go out and seek, not here in London or in the houses of pleasure, for someone you will love and who will love you, not because you are important but because you are a man and she is a woman."

"That is what we all want," the Earl murmured.

"You are right to want that and to seek for it, my boy. And so to make it interesting I am going to make the chase more exciting by proposing that I will give a prize to you who are here today if you fall in love with your ideal woman and she accepts your offer of marriage not knowing who you are."

"*Not knowing who we are?*" the Marquis enquired.

"Exactly what I say, you go on your search without your title and without anything to make those you meet aware that you are different from any ordinary man with the exception that you are a gentleman."

There was a gasp of surprise from everybody.

"To those of you who find what you are seeking," the Duke went on, "and who bring the woman they have discovered back to meet me, I will make him a present of one thousand pounds which would surely start the marriage in the comfort you are all accustomed to!"

"One thousand pounds!" the Earl exclaimed. "That is certainly a very generous prize, Your Grace."

"Fortunately I can afford it. I will not be depriving my heirs as I have always invested my money wisely with the good sense I chose my wife. That is what I am asking you young bucks to do."

He smiled at them all as he carried on,

"Instead of talking about it here and drinking far too early in the morning, you should ride out like Knights in the past, seeking the unexpected and adventure. I can promise that practically every one of you will find it."

"You are very generous, Your Grace," the Marquis said, "and for the moment you have taken my breath away. As far as I am concerned, I accept your bet. But you have not told me what we pay *you* if we lose."

The Duke laughed.

"If you lost, then the stipulation is you are married within the year and if you yourself have not found the right woman, you have to accept one chosen by your family. Then you can only hope and pray she will develop as the years progress into one of the attractive married ladies you have just been praising so highly."

They chuckled as they recalled their earlier words.

"There is no reason to accept my offer. I only ask that before you set off on this wild exciting adventure you are kind enough to drop your card through my front door.

"There is no need for explanations or for anyone to know what you are doing. Just leave me your name and I will know that you have set forth to seek the greatest prize of all – the real love and affection for a woman you love because she is yours."

As the Duke finished speaking, he loooked at them all individually before saying,

"I bid you goodday, gentlemen, and good hunting!"

With that he walked across the smoking room and the Marquis ran after him to escort him to the door.

As the porter fetched the Duke's hat and walking cane, the Marquis said,

"You have certainly given us much to think about, Your Grace. I myself find it quite impossible not to accept your wager. I intend to set off tomorrow morning."

"I thought you would find it irresistible, Ivor," he smiled. "I cannot help feeling that somehow even if it seems like a miracle you will find what you are seeking."

"I do so hope you are right, Your Grace, but it is undoubtedly a challenge no man who calls himself a man could resist."

"That is what I thought when I came and spoke to you. I am sure that if nothing else, it will give your friends a new outlook on life you are not likely to find in London."

As he was speaking his closed carriage drawn by two horses had come to the front door. The Duke walked down the steps and across the pavement. He then climbed into his carriage and the footman closed the door.

He bent forward to raise his hand to the Marquis as the carriage drove off.

He walked back into the smoking room to find his friends talking excitedly amongst themselves.

They had at first been stunned by the Duke's offer and now each of them was asking where they could go.

How would it be possible to travel without a valet or groom to enable them to remain anonymous?

As the Marquis joined them, the Earl exclaimed,

"How can it be possible for this to happen to us so unexpectedly without us having the slightest idea that the Duke was listening to our conversation?"

"I didn't realise he was there. At the same time he has challenged us in a way that is quite irresistible."

"I agree with you," the Earl added. "I will only be scared I cannot find this mythical and wonderful woman to fall in love with. In which case I will be obliged to marry some creature my family will provide."

His last words were laced with sarcasm and Lord Dromont laughed and parried,

"You would be no worse off than you are at the moment. You know as I do that your father is desperate for you to be married simply because he just loathes your cousin who will inherit the title if you die without a son."

"As my cousin is double my age," the young Lord replied, "I think that unlikely!"

"You never know," the Marquis interjected. "You might lose your life in a duel or be run over by a phaeton!"

The Earl then came in,

"Frankly I think the whole idea is very amusing, and we have nothing to lose by it. A thousand pounds if we win and if we lose, the position remains exactly as it is now and we will each have to marry someone our family has chosen for us."

"That is true," the Marquis agreed. "Anyway it will be an adventure which at least will prevent us from being bored as we so often are."

"You speak for yourself," the Earl responded. "I am entranced by a little charmer at the moment who dances divinely and who I have just installed at considerable cost in a secluded house in Chelsea."

"You can bet one thing," said Lord Dromont, "she will not wait for you if you are away. That is the trouble I have always found with those entrancing 'soiled doves'."

They all laughed and then one of them chipped in,

"Personally I will be glad to leave London. I find it extremely expensive and I am continually complaining I do not get a proper return for my money."

"As I see it," the Marquis said, "if we have to be completely anonymous we must set off alone on horseback and just hope the adventure the Duke has promised us will drop down from the sky or rise from the waters of a pool."

"If you are looking for nymphs and mermaids you are not likely to find them," another put in. "Personally I will keep to the high road. I feel certain the pretty unspoilt girls we are looking for will be found in country villages."

"That is certainly a point, Gerald, but we will each have to map out our own journey and just hope the Duke is right in suggesting that there are beautiful creatures in the countryside."

"Well, we can but start off hopefully on what may prove to be an absolutely hopeless and ridiculous journey."

"You can always stay at home, Freddie, and hope that someone who is more concerned with your heart than your title will fall down the chimney!"

"I suppose we all hope that," was the reply. "At the same time I am doubtful, very doubtful, if these beautiful, intelligent and unspoilt girls we seek really exist – if you ask me the only place to find them is in a book or on the stage at Drury Lane!"

Everyone laughed as the Marquis suggested,

"I think we should time ourselves. If our search is not complete in three or six months, whichever you desire, we should give up the chase and accept our obligation to marry a woman our family deems appropriate for us."

"Well, give us time to breathe. Three months is not long enough. You can be quite certain the women we are seeking are unlikely to fall like manna from Heaven!"

"I am aware of that, but all of us have obligations and frankly I would not like to leave my estate and horses for longer than three months."

There was a murmur and then one of them sighed,

"All right, Ivor, you win. We will make it three months and if we do have to get married to some ghastly creature after that we can very likely make her take another three months or more buying her trousseau!"

"I personally am betting on us all finding what we seek and that goes for you too, Tony. So we will all meet here exactly three months from today and the Duke shall be our guest. I can only hope it costs him a great deal of money as we will have all been successful."

The Marquis spoke optimistically, but he did feel it was most unlikely he would find what he was seeking.

He was not really very certain what it was as he had never yet found a woman he was so much in love with that he felt he could not live without her.

Of course there had been women in his life but they had mostly been married women – they had been amusing, witty and very flirtatious and who had willingly given him their favours when their husbands were away.

Because the Duke was well read and intelligent he already knew that this was not enough and although the Marquis resented the way his family interfered with him, he knew at the back of his mind they were right.

He had to marry sooner or later.

He had to have an heir.

And the only question up to now had been – with whom?

CHAPTER TWO

After luncheon was over the Marquis drove back from White's to his house in Berkeley Square, which was a large and impressive building at one end of the Square.

He was thinking as he drove his phaeton with great dexterity that he would miss his team when he left London.

All through luncheon they had, of course, talked of nothing but the challenge from the Duke of Sandelford.

Every man had a different idea of where he should go, which the Marquis felt was a good omen as it would be a mistake for two of them to be searching the same part of the country for the ultimate prize – they might end up with the same girl and that would cause trouble!

Equally he felt that if they were all disillusioned and found it impossible to find anyone to please them, the Duke would be disappointed and would feel he had sent them all out on a wild goose chase.

As far as the Marquis himself was concerned, he felt the whole project needed a good deal of planning.

When he arrived at Berkeley Square he sent for his secretary as he needed to know what engagements he had agreed to for the next few weeks.

He was horrified to find he had accepted invitations for nearly every day until the end of the month and there was a pile of even more that had not yet received a reply.

His secretary was waiting for answers.

"I have to go away for a bit, Harrison," the Marquis told him, "and leave you in charge of the correspondence.

You will have to be tactful in making them aware that you do not know where I am or the date I will be returning."

Mr. Harrison who had been with the Marquis for some years was shocked.

"But you have accepted all these parties, my Lord," he protested, "so they will be exceedingly disappointed if you don't turn up at the last moment."

"It is not a question of the last moment, Harrison. I will be leaving tomorrow or the next day for the country. You will be unable to get in touch with me until I return."

"But your Lordship has no idea of the engagements you have ahead of you."

"I know they are all for parties which will be very like each other. I cannot believe I am indispensable! What you must do, Harrison, is placate them with apologies and flowers for the hostesses. If it is necessary send a case of champagne or the best port to the host."

Mr. Harrison made a helpless gesture.

"I'll try to carry out your orders, my Lord, but it will not be easy, especially when your close friends wish to be in touch with you urgently."

"It is one thing they just cannot do because I am not certain where I will be myself. All I will do is to return as soon as I can and you will just have to smooth the troubled waters until I do."

Mr. Harrison sighed but did not reply.

The Marquis then dictated a number of letters to his closest friends saying he had been called away, but would let them know immediately when he returned to London.

He was thinking he had finished when his secretary blurted out,

"What about His Royal Highness, my Lord?"

The Marquis drew in his breath.

He had completely forgotten that the Prince Regent was expecting him at his next party at Carlton House and he invariably relied on his close friends to help when he threw one of his large and to him extravagent parties.

The Marquis was thinking how he should inform His Royal Highness that he would not be available.

If he sent a note to him before he left, the Prince Regent would undoubtedly forbid him to be away for more than a week and he would make it a Royal command so that he would be unable to refuse.

"I think the best thing," he said after a long pause, "would be to wait until His Royal Highness sends for me urgently. Then you must go to Carlton House and explain that you have no idea where I am and it is thus absolutely impossible for you to obey his instructions."

Mr. Harrison sighed.

"It's not something I'll look forward to, my Lord."

"I know that, Harrison, but you have to help me and only you can prevent there being either a hue-and-cry for me or many speculations as to why I *had* to leave."

"Is that the truth, my Lord?"

"No, it is not. I am leaving of my own free will and for your information and yours alone, I have been given a challenge which is so important to my life now and in the future that I just cannot refuse it."

Mr. Harrison's eyes were alive with curiosity.

"A challenge, my Lord. That sounds exciting!"

"I only hope it will be exciting, but to tell the truth, Harrison, I rather doubt if I will be successful."

"I'll certainly do everything possible to help while your Lordship's away, but you cannot blame me for hoping it'll not be for long."

"I feel the same, Harrison, but just now I will only concern myself with what I need for my journey and it is your job to keep curious eyes away from the front door."

Mr. Harrison laughed as he knew only too well that there would be a commotion when it was discovered that the Marquis had left without giving anyone an address.

However, there was nothing more he could say, so he merely produced the morning post.

There was a letter in a coloured scented envelope headed '*Private*' and he passed it to the Marquis unopened.

He put it on one side to look at all his other letters first and it was over an hour later when Mr. Harrison had left him that the Marquis opened the blue envelope.

It was fragrant with a scent he recognised at once.

As he pulled the letter out, he knew without even glancing at the signature who it was from.

"*My darling wonderful Ivor,*" he read. "*Arthur is leaving this afternoon and will not be returning until late tomorrow.*

I will be alone and longing for you at ten o'clock if I can escape early from the party at Bedlington House."

The Marquis read the letter through twice and then he thought he might as well accept the invitation before he left for the country.

He had been having an *affaire-de-coeur* with the writer – the Countess of Claremont.

She was one of the great Social beauties of the day and there was not a man in London who did not thrill when she smiled at him.

Red-haired and green-eyed she had taken the Social world by storm and she was undoubtedly the belle of every ball she attended.

The Marquis had flirted with her when they first danced together and he was delighted when, on receiving an invitation to Claremont House, she greeted him alone.

They dined, not in the great State dining room, but in her boudoir and it was quite obvious what she expected of him when dinner was over and the servants withdrew.

He had learnt before he arrived that her husband was attending a race meeting in Somerset.

The door into her bedroom led, he had thought at the time, into a paradise that had been closed to a great number of other men.

Lovemaking with the Countess was wildly exciting and more fiery than anything he had known in his life.

Their liaison had continued but it was not an easy one. The Earl was extremely jealous and well aware of his wife's beauty and desirability, so he seldom left her alone.

To say that the Marquis was infatuated would be to exaggerate the effect the Countess had on him.

He found her utterly desirable as any man would as she was so beautiful and sensuous, but he had made love to many women and after his first delight at being chosen as her lover, he found that there was nothing really different in their lovemaking than with other beauties.

She was sweet and she was beautiful and she found him without any doubt one of her most ardent lovers.

"I must see you. I *must* see you again," she purred the last time they had been together.

"I am waiting for you to tell me exactly when that is possible," replied the Marquis.

"Arthur very seldom goes away without me," she sighed. "You know, Ivor, I want you, I want you!"

"And I want you too, Juno, but we cannot do the impossible and so I can only wait outside your front door until you are alone."

"Supposing I came to you," she had said suddenly.

"It would be a big mistake. However carefully we might arrange it, people passing my house would see your carriage outside the door and however we may trust them, servants invariably talk."

"Of course you are right," she had sighed. "But I need you and I want you! It seems an eternity since we were last together."

The Marquis had been too sensible to take risks and although it had been hushed up, it was well-known that her husband had already challenged two men to a duel.

And the one thing the Marquis had been told by his father for whom he had a great respect, was that there must never be a scandal connected to the Milvertons.

He had therefore known that trying though it might be, he must not approach the Countess – at least not until it was an occasion when they would not be interrupted and the Earl too far away to be a threat.

He had found the Countess's complaints somewhat boring as he danced with her at parties and she would say over and over again as they did so,

"I want you! I so want you, Ivor and I lie awake at night hoping and praying you are thinking of me and not of any other women."

This was of course very flattering at first, but after a time the Marquis found it increasingly tedious.

If the Countess was not available there was always someone almost as lovely waiting for him with open arms.

*

Now as he read her letter again he thought perhaps it would not only be a kindness but a rather dramatic way of saying goodbye to his old life.

If he found this wonderful girl in whom the Duke believed, there would be no question in the future of lovely Countesses – or any other beauty who had been acclaimed by the *Beau Monde* as irresistible.

'I wonder if it will be possible for me to be faithful to one woman for the rest of my life?' the Marquis asked himself frequently.

Then he remembered what his father and mother had told him was the basis of a perfect marriage, but then somehow he could not believe it would happen to himself – yet in a way it was what he wanted.

'Perhaps,' he mused, 'in saying goodbye to Juno, I will say goodbye to the *Beau Monde* and all its endless temptations.'

As he was ruminating he could almost see a row of women he had found desirable these last five years.

None of them had very lasted long – they had been exciting, lovely and amusing, but as he thought back it was they who had opened the door to an affair – and invariably it had been he who had closed it.

He could not explain to himself why a beauty who he had found utterly desirable could suddenly and for no reason cease to attract him, yet he had to admit this sudden end of an *affaire-de-coeur* had happened many times.

Always at his instigation, not hers.

'Juno is different,' he told himself. 'Therefore just in case I find what I am seeking I must say goodbye to her. I want her to remember me with affection – not with tears and reproaches.'

He read Juno's letter for the fourth time and then he tore it into minute pieces.

He did not answer her letter as he knew she would not expect a reply in writing. She would be quite certain, because no man had ever refused her that he would dine with her as requested.

It was later in the afternoon before the Marquis sent for Mr. Harrison and asked him where he was supposed to be dining this evening.

"You surely have not forgotten, my Lord, that you accepted an invitation to dine at Devonshire House."

"Send a messenger with this letter," he ordered as he sat down and wrote a letter of apology to the Duchess.

He said he had been called to the country as one of his relatives was desperately ill and asking for him and it was a call he could not refuse.

He was in fact certain he would hardly be missed as the parties at Devonshire House were always very big with at least thirty guests all being entertained with a delicious meal in the gigantic dining room.

It was the sort of evening the Marquis always found amusing and he would have undoubtedly enjoyed himself, but if he had to say goodbye to Juno for ever he could not miss this opportunity of being alone with her.

Now having cleared the decks he thought he must think of where he would go tomorrow.

It was obvious that he must make a start from his country house in Hertfordshire.

He would undoubtedly have a better mount to ride from there than he would if he left from London. His fine stables and the horses that gave him the greatest pleasure were all at Milverton Hall.

There was no one staying there at the moment and he had been with his mother at her house in Essex before he had returned to London yesterday.

It was at Milverton Hall his relatives would gather and they merely wanted to force him to listen once again to their pleas that he should marry.

Because he had spent so much time in London he had recently rather neglected the Hall.

He thought now it was where he should start from, although he had no idea where he was going.

However, he told his valet that he would want some rather plain ordinary clothes to wear while he was away.

"Most of them be in the country already, my Lord," the valet volunteered. "You're always 'dressed up to kill' when you be in London, so I just leaves all your Lordship's more comfortable things down there."

As he changed for dinner he told his valet that they would be leaving first thing in the morning and therefore he would have to pack everything he would need tonight.

His valet who had been with him many years said,

"A bit strange for your Lordship to be going to the country just when things be a-buzzing here. Do you, my Lord, reckon of being there long?"

"Not as far as I am concerned, Croft, but I will tell you more when we reach Milverton Hall."

Croft looked surprised but merely muttered,

"Very good, my Lord," and began packing.

At the same time he was wondering to himself what could have happened now to take his Lordship back to the country and he knew as well as Mr. Harrison did that his Lordship had a long list of engagements ahead of him.

The Marquis had ordered his closed carriage to be outside for him at a quarter-to-eight.

Precisely at that time he walked downstairs looking exceedingly smart in his cutaway evening coat with tails.

His neckpiece was in the latest and most intricate fashion and the points of his collar were high on his neck.

24

The footmen watching him thought no gentleman in the Social world could look smarter or at the same time so unmistakably masculine.

The Marquis then stepped into his carriage and the butler and the footmen bowed as he drove off.

He told the coachman to set him down in what he knew was an empty house three doors away from where the Countess lived.

She had given him a key and so he let himself in to a dark and dismal hall until his carriage had driven away.

He thought at the time it was very sensible of her, but he still could not help wondering how many men had been given the key before him.

Yet the first time he had used it he thought only of the rapture that was waiting for him a few doors down the Square as he gazed through the shutters at his carriage until it was out of sight.

Now, as he had often done before, he went out of the house, locked it and put the key in his pocket and then he walked on to Claremont House.

The butler who let him in intoned respectfully,

"It's very good to see your Lordship again."

The Marquis nodded and as he knew what would come next, he waited until the butler added,

"Her Ladyship's a little tired this evening, my Lord, and thought your Lordship'd understand if you had dinner in her boudoir. It would save her coming downstairs."

"I think it very wise of her Ladyship not to do more than is absolutely necessary," replied the Marquis.

He could not help recalling it was a conversation he had in exactly the same words on his last visit, but he had already been told that the old butler adored his Mistress and could be trusted.

He followed the man up the stairs and as he opened the door of the boudoir the butler said in a stentorian tone,

"The Marquis of Milverton, my Lady."

The Marquis stepped forward.

As he expected the Countess was wearing a most seductive gown and she rose from the sofa where she had been reclining.

The room was resplendent with bouquets of flowers and their scent mingled with the exotic perfume used by the Countess – it was one the Marquis was very familiar with and it stayed on his skin long after he had left her.

"Ivor, how kind of you to come when I was alone, and so lonely!" exclaimed the Countess.

Then as the butler shut the door she flung her arms round the Marquis's neck crying as she did so,

"*You are here*! I was so afraid you would not come as I so longed you to."

"Of course I came, Juno, and it seems ages since we have been together."

"It has been a thousand years, but now you are here and nothing else matters. Oh, my darling, wonderful Ivor, I have missed you so!"

Her lips were lifted to his and as he kissed her he knew that the fires were already burning within him.

After a delicious dinner served in the boudoir the Marquis sat back in his chair.

There was his favourite liqueur in his hand and he thought only the Countess was clever enough to entertain him in such a glamorous style without it appearing in any way questionable.

All the other women with whom he had an *affaire-de-coeur* had asked him to dine with their friends and after dinner they would make a great palaver that their carriage had not arrived – and so the Marquis would offer them a lift home and then he stayed behind.

Otherwise he would dine at White's or at home and then he would then go to their house at ten o'clock when the majority of servants would have retired to bed.

When this happened he usually let himself in with a key that had been provided for him or a door was left open by a lady's maid.

"Your husband does not mind you inviting me?" the Marquis had asked the Countess on their first evening.

Juno had smiled at him.

"I don't tell him we are alone. I merely say I had a dinner party and you were one of the guests."

She gave a little laugh.

"The great secret is when you deceive always tell the truth as much as possible. The less you have to hide the less worrying it is – "

The Marquis had agreed with her philosophy and he actually found it better to do exactly as she suggested.

He thought no one could be as pretty or actually the right word was glorious as his hostess.

She had been amusing and all through dinner had made him laugh and it was only when their eyes met and there was a sudden silence between them that the Marquis knew what she was thinking.

Now they moved from the table to the sofa while the servants cleared away the dishes. She was showing the Marquis some of the drawings that had been done of her by a well known artist.

He had said, as was expected, that they were good, but not good enough.

"Will that be everything, my Lady?" the butler now enquired.

"Everything, thank you, Barker. His Lordship will let himself out, so there is no need for a footman on duty. I know they have had a long week."

"That's very gracious of your Ladyship."

Barker bowed and left the room.

Then as the door closed behind him, the Countess held out her arms to the Marquis.

"At last!" she cried. "I have missed you! Oh, how I have missed you, Ivor!"

"And I have missed you too, Juno."

He sought her lips but she slipped away from him.

"What are you waiting for?" she asked him as she opened the door that led into her bedroom.

As he followed her the Marquis saw that the room was dark, except for a small candelabra with three candles by the big muslin-curtained bed.

He closed the door behind him and as he did so the Countess placed her arms around his neck.

"I love you! I love you," she whispered. "I have been waiting an eternity for this moment."

The Marquis kissed her and then she began to slip off her flowing gown.

He too undressed in a dark corner of the room and when he reached her there were only two candles burning beside the bed.

But there was no need to light his way to her.

She was holding out her arms and her fair hair was falling softly over her naked shoulders.

Then all the fires within her leapt still higher as the Marquis's lips came down on hers.

*

It was two hours later that the Marquis thought it was time he returned home.

For a moment they were both silent and exhausted from the passion that had enveloped them.

He thought Juno was asleep, but when he moved to the edge of the bed she put out her hand to prevent him.

"You are not leaving me?" she purred.

"I think it's time for me to go. Actually I am going to the country early tomorrow morning. Therefore I don't want to be too tired."

"To the country!" she exclaimed. "But you cannot go away now! Surely I can see you tomorrow evening? Arthur will not be returning until Thursday."

The Marquis, however, moved across the room to the dark corner where he had left his clothes.

He was wondering as he did so whether he should perhaps postpone his departure to the country – what had happened tonight had been so enjoyable.

But he knew it was always a mistake to try to repeat anything so pleasant and it might be a disappointment the second time.

The Countess sat up in the bed.

"You cannot go away tomorrow! What a ridiculous idea! Besides you can never leave London when there are so many amusing parties."

"I know that," replied the Marquis, as he buttoned up his shirt. "But I have arranged to go first to Milverton Hall. Then I am not quite sure when it will be possible for me to return to London."

"But, my darling Ivor, we may not have this chance again. You know how Arthur hates travelling and it was, I thought, a Heaven sent opportunity that he should have left me just at this moment."

She sighed before she finished,

"Usually he wants to be in attendance on His Royal Highness or drag me to every ball. It may be weeks before he goes away again, so you must stay! *You must*!"

There was now a strong note in her voice and it told him all too clearly that she was going to be difficult.

This had happened often and he always found it an unpleasant argument that he wished to avoid at all costs.

"I will do my best to come to you," he murmured.

"You must! *You must*! You really must! How can I live without you? Why do you leave me now, Ivor, it is still quite early?"

"As I have told you, Juno, I have a journey to make tomorrow. If I have to put it off, there will be problems."

He put on his coat and then he slipped his tie into his pocket rather than arrange it.

Unexpectedly there was a knock at the door.

Both the Countess and the Marquis stiffened.

"Who is there? What do you want?" the Countess called out after a pause.

"His Lordship's just arriving, my Lady," came a muffled voice.

The Countess gave a little cry of horror.

"It's Arthur!" she now wailed. "He has come back deliberately. I was half-afraid he might do so, yet I was sure he did not suspect you."

The Marquis walked swiftly across the room.

"How do I get out of here?" he demanded.

"There is only the one window," she whispered. "It may be dangerous, but it is not a very long drop to the roof of the kitchen."

The Marquis did not hesitate.

He pulled aside the curtains and saw through the window that there was a flat top to the building below.

There was a water pipe that he felt he could hold on to as he descended, rather than to jump straight down as the Countess was suggesting.

He did not wait, but put his leg over the windowsill and even as he did so, he heard the door of the bedroom rasp open behind him.

"*Arthur*!"

The Countess's voice was shrill and rang out.

"What a lovely surprise! I had no idea you would get away so soon. Oh, darling! It's wonderful to see you!"

The Marquis started to slide slowly and carefully down the water pipe.

He realised that behind him the Countess had flung her arms round her husband.

"I am so thrilled to see you, I am really!" she was saying. "To me it's a marvellous, marvellous suprise that you have come back."

"I have come back for other reasons besides seeing you," the Earl responded in a deep voice. "Who has been here with you this evening?"

The Marquis had almost reached the flat roof over the kitchen and he could still hear as the window was open what was being said inside the bedroom.

"I had two friends to dinner," the Countess replied. "It was very dull without you, my darling husband, and I was glad when they left me."

"Are you quite sure they left you?" the Earl snarled. "I am going to look for myself."

"Don't be ridiculous!" the Countess expostulated.

The Marquis realised she was holding her husband back from going to the window.

He looked around him desperately and it was then he recognised that he had slipped down on the far side of the roof. There was a space between this house and the wall of the one next door.

With the swiftness of a man who was athletic and quick-witted, he hurled himself over the side of the roof.

He dropped down without hurting himself, but at the same time he knocked over a dustbin that fell with a crash to the ground.

He was in the shadows and he dared not look up in case the Earl staring out of the window above could see the top of his head.

The contents of the dustbin spilled and they smelt most unpleasant, but still he waited with his head down, pressing himself as close as he could against the wall.

Then he could hear above him the Countess saying,

"What are you looking for, Arthur? You can see there is no one about at this time of night."

"What was that noise I have just heard?" he asked.

"I expect it's those beastly cats again," she replied. "They woke me up the night before last. I told the cook to keep the dustbins covered. They were obviously struggling to eat what had been thrown out."

There was silence.

The Marquis was certain that the Earl was looking in every direction expecting to see him or some other man moving quickly away.

"Oh, do stop looking out of the window and come to bed," he heard the Countess say. "There is nothing to see at this time of night."

The Marquis could not see them, but he was certain that the Earl was again looking in every direction. He was obviously suspicious yet at present he could see no one he could point a finger at.

The Marquis did not move. The smell from the dustbin made him want to cough, but he forced himself to be silent.

Then, almost as if he was watching them, he was aware that the Earl had moved from the window and he could hear the Countess's voice although he could not make out what she was saying.

She was talking in a soft and seductive voice to her husband and he was answering her briefly. But he was no longer looking out of the bedroom window.

Very carefully the Marquis peeped up and saw that the curtains were now closed.

He knew it would be fatal to make any noise, so moving over the rubbish that covered the ground from the dustbin he managed to make his way out of the alley.

Now he was in the Mews behind the house and he knew, however, that it would be a mistake to walk through the empty Mews – the risk was still there that the Earl might once again look out of the window.

It was so late or rather so early in the morning that there was a moon overhead and the stars filled the sky.

Any man walking alone up the empty Mews would be a suspect, so keeping his back to the wall and his head down the Marquis managed to squeeze his way along the back of the house.

Finally he reached the door that led into the kitchen quarters and as he let himself out into the street, he heaved a sigh of relief.

He knew if the Earl had the slightest indication he was actually there, he would have challenged him at once to a duel.

Duels were frowned on by the authorities and not supposed to take place. Yet it was a challenge he would be forced as a gentleman to accept and there was no doubt that the Earl was an exceptionally good shot.

Although he was suspicious he had no evidence. He had no doubt been told that his wife was betraying him, but he had to substantiate it.

As the Marquis walked back to Berkeley Square, he told himself,

'If there is no other reason for me to be leaving London tomorrow, I now have the perfect excuse for going to the country and staying there!'

CHAPTER THREE

The Marquis left London early in the morning and driving his fastest phaeton with three horses he reached his country home, Milverton Hall, in under three hours.

This was not a record because he had made it faster with a chaise, but he was delighted with his new team.

His valet and luggage were following in a trap and they would inevitably take longer.

On his arrival he was thrilled to see how beautiful Milverton Hall was looking and the garden was ablaze with colour. Although he had not been home for some time, he knew that everything would be in perfect order.

As the Marquis drove up the drive, he thought that he really must spend more time than he had recently at the family house. It was unique and had been owned by the Milvertons for over three hundred years.

He had a sudden impulse not to take up the Duke's challenge and instead he would stay at the Hall and enjoy himself with his thoroughbreds.

He decided that before he set out on his adventure in search of a wife, he must spend a few days in the stables.

When he was driving down from London and had given the horses their heads, he had thought over what had happened to him last night and it made him feel that, for the moment, he was fed up with London and only too well aware, apart from the danger of a duel if the Earl had found him, of the scandal that would have hurt his whole family.

He considered now that he had been very stupid.

He should not have continued his *affaire-de-coeur* with the Countess for so long. Everyone in London knew that the Earl was exceedingly jealous and the Marquis felt now that he had been saved by a miracle.

He should be very grateful that he was not facing a furious family and risking his life in Green Park tomorrow morning at first light.

He wanted to swear never to go into an *affaire-de-coeur* with a married woman again – but he realised that was tempting fate.

If he saw a woman who was particularly beautiful, she would be irresistible and he would then undoubtedly try, as he had tried with the Countess, to enjoy himself and not get caught!

As the Marquis halted his team at the front door the sun was shining on the windows of the Hall and the light made him feel that the house was welcoming him home.

Equally it was as much a part of his family and so he felt it was also telling him that he must provide an heir.

It was a message he did not wish to hear, so he then pulled his horses in rather sharply because it disturbed him.

The front door opened and two footmen rolled out a red carpet and the Marquis saw Newman, the old butler, who had been at the Hall since he had been a small boy.

Running from the stables were two grooms to go to the heads of his horses and the Marquis fastened his reins and climbed down.

He spoke to his Head Groom who was delighted to hear he had completed his journey in so short a time.

Then as he walked up the steps on the red carpet Newman was waiting for him at the top.

"Welcome home, my Lord," he proclaimed. "It's a long time we've been waiting for you. We're real glad that your Lordship's not forgotten us."

"I never forget you, Newman. It is just that I have been busy in London and paying a visit to my mother."

"I hope her Ladyship's in good health, my Lord. She is sadly missed in the villages."

"I thought she would be but as you know, Newman, she has a number of her relatives near her where she lives now and she might find it rather lonely here."

As he was speaking he handed his hat and gloves to a footman and then he walked towards the study.

Newman followed him and added quickly,

"I think I should tell your Lordship that your aunt, Lady Matilda Fletcher, is here."

"Lady Matilda!" the Marquis exclaimed. "What is she doing here and why was I not informed?"

"Her Ladyship only arrived last night and she was, I believe, on her way to London. But when she hears your Lordship was coming today, she was ever so glad."

"I am sure she was," the Marquis said sarcastically. "Is she alone?"

Newman hesitated for a moment.

"No, my Lord! She brings a young lady with her."

The Marquis stared at his butler.

Then with some effort he prevented himself from exclaiming the words on the tip of his tongue.

Instead he asked,

"Where is her Ladyship now, Newman?"

"In the study, my Lord. She was very certain your Lordship'd go there first."

If there was one relative he really disliked it was his father's elder sister, Lady Matilda Fletcher. She had always been someone who criticised and interfered with whatever any family member was doing.

The Marquis was quite certain he knew now why she was chasing him. She had been unable to be present at the party his mother gave for him.

Practically every relative who had come to it had a suggestion as to who he should marry.

He was therefore quite certain that his Aunt Matilda would not rest until she had put forward her protégé.

It was obviously some tiresome girl he had no wish to meet and just for a moment he wondered if he could avoid Aunt Matilda by staying somewhere else.

In which case she might well travel on to London to look for him.

Then he told himself it was too late.

Newman opened the door and the Marquis walked into the study where Aunt Matilda was waiting for him

As he had expected, his aunt was looking somewhat more aggressive than usual.

She was sitting bolt-upright on the edge of the sofa and beside her was, the Marquis thought at a quick glance, a rather plain young girl.

Lady Matilda held out her hand.

"Oh, here you are, Ivor," she huffed. "I guessed that you would make the journey from London in record time. Edith and I have been waiting for you."

The Marquis noticed that she gave the girl beside her a slight push and then she rose to her feet, but she was rather clumsy about it.

He reckoned she was slightly fat and her dull brown hair only just reached her shoulders.

"Now shake hands, Edith," Lady Matilda ordered in a sharp voice. "This is my nephew, the Marquis, who I told you about. I am sure he has heard of your father."

The Marquis took the somewhat limp hand that was outstretched to him as Lady Matilda droned on,

"Edith's father is Lord Basildon, whose brilliant speeches in the House of Lords have been reported in all the newspapers. I am sure even when you were away from London, Ivor, that you must have read about them."

The Marquis was not the least interested in politics, however he remembered vaguely that there was indeed such a person as Lord Basildon. He seldom bothered to read the speeches from the House of Lords as the majority of them were so incredibly dull.

"I am so very sorry I was unable to come to see you when you were staying with your mother," Lady Matilda was saying. "I had already written to her to say that I was anxious for you to meet dear Edith, as I was in fact taking the girl to London."

She paused and realised that the Marquis was not listening. He had moved to the writing table.

"I am talking to you, Ivor!" his aunt said sharply.

"I am listening to you, Aunt Matilda, but I was just looking to see if there was any correspondence here which might be of urgency. It is where it is always left if there is something I must know as soon as I arrive home."

He was not mistaken as there was a piece of paper on the table and when he opened it he read,

"*Skylark gave birth to an excellent foal yesterday. The grooms are hoping your Lordship will have time to see it while you are here.*"

The Marquis was delighted. He had purchased the mare from a friend who had assured him that any foal she might carry would undoubtedly be a winner.

'I will certainly see it before I leave,' he decided.

Then with difficulty he forced himself to attend to Lady Matilda who was still thundering on.

"What I have been hoping you might do," she said, "is give a ball for Edith when we are in London. Her father says that he is too old to know all the young people who should be asked for such an occasion."

She smiled at him sweetly before she added,

"But I am sure, dear Ivor, you know all the young gentlemen who frequent the smart balls that make every Season so outstanding."

The Marquis was instinctly alert that this ruse was another way of trapping him.

Just how on earth could he give a ball for any girl, especially one who was not a relative?

Every gossip in the *Beau Monde* would spring to the conclusion that he intended to marry her and *that* he recognised only too well was what his aunt was planning.

"Of course I would hate," he smiled at her, "not to do anything you wanted me to do, Aunt Matilda. But I am actually going away on a special visit and I am not certain when I shall be back in London."

"How can you possibly leave London in the middle of the Season!" cried Lady Matilda.

Her voice was almost a scream.

"Very easily as it happens, I have broken the record coming here and tomorrow I will be leaving so you have only just – as you might easily say – caught me in time."

"Now what could be more important to you than to be in London just when all the balls are taking place, Ivor. I am sure His Royal Highness will be giving one of his magnificent parties. How could he do so without you?"

"I expect he will manage! But, as I have no idea when I shall return, it's no use counting on me. Now if you will forgive me I must go to get ready for luncheon."

He walked over to the door and left the room before Lady Matilda could think of a way to detain him further.

He ran up the stairs to the Master bedroom where he had slept ever since his father died.

As he did so he thought it was just what he might have expected. Whatever was going on in the family his Aunt Matilda always upset it – she had different ideas and different ambitions to all his other relatives.

'If she thinks I am so stupid as to marry the girl she has just produced,' the Marquis mused, 'she is very much mistaken.'

He remembered now that Lord Basildon came from an ancient aristocratic family and was exceedingly rich and the rather plain young woman was therefore the girl his family would think an ideal wife for him.

She would undoubtedly do everything in her power to make him – what she would call – see sense!

'I wish the old women would leave me alone!' the Marquis murmured. 'It would be just what they deserve if on the Duke's wild goose chase some girl without any blue blood and a rough background insisted on marrying me!'

The idea amused him.

He thought just how furious his relatives and Aunt Matilda would be, but he was sure that anyone was better than the girls considered desirable by his aunts and uncles.

Luncheon was an excellent meal as the cook who adored the Marquis since he had been a boy, had produced at no more than a moment's notice, all his favourite dishes.

The Marquis sat at the top of the table with his aunt on his right and Edith Basildon on his left.

41

Her Ladyship insisted on talking, as she always did, all through the luncheon and the Marquis thought as they finished that Edith had not been able to utter one word.

He therefore said kindly to her and it was the first sentence he had spoken to her directly,

"Do you enjoy the country?"

"I-I have never lived – anywhere – else," replied Edith in a small voice.

"I expect you enjoy riding?"

There was a little pause before the girl answered,

"Only if the horse is particularly quiet. I should be frightened to ride a strange horse. Although Lady Matilda has told me your stables are famous."

"I like to think they are. They are certainly very precious to me. Therefore you must forgive me if I leave you to go to visit my horses."

He was making his excuses early before he found it impossible to stand any more of his aunt's conversation as she was trying to impress him with Edith's background – it was all quite unnecessary and exceedingly boring.

The Marquis knew of old how her mind worked. She was steadily getting round to the right moment when she would ask him face to face if he would marry Edith.

The answer was a guaranteed '*no!*' but he found it easier to run away.

"We will have tea ready in the drawing room later," Lady Matilda called out as he reached the door.

"If I am late, don't wait for me," he answered and went out before she could reply.

He ran down the steps and up towards the stables knowing that the Head Groom would be expecting him.

His horses were looking fine and better than when he had last seen them. One, he was informed, was a better jumper than expected and there was another the grooms were certain would win the steeplechase if he entered for it.

He took a long time talking about every horse and inspecting them all, moving from stall to stall.

"Which horse do you want to ride now, my Lord?" the Head Groom asked after the Marquis had spent nearly two hours in the stables.

Because he knew it would please them, he chose the stallion the grooms had selected for the steeplechase, named Firefly, and when he was mounted, he realised that he could not have chosen better himself.

He gave the horse its head on the flat ground and then he took him over several jumps. There was no doubt he had a winner and he smiled to himself as he rode on.

In fact the whole afternoon was a delight.

When the Marquis eventually arrived back at the Hall it was long after teatime and he reckoned that if his aunt and her protégé had waited for him, they would surely be hungry.

At the same time the sooner he left the better.

If indeed he was really to go on this mad adventure devised by the Duke, he himself should be the first past the winning post.

If he failed he knew one thing – he would not marry Edith Basildon, however good her antecedents might be!

Newman told him that the ladies had waited tea for some time and then her Ladyship had gone upstairs to rest.

"And where is Miss Basildon?"

"She's out in the garden, my Lord."

The Marquis thought in that case he could go to the study and he gave Newman instructions to say he had no idea where he was.

He sat down to look over the reports from the farms which he knew would be waiting for him. They were more interesting than he had expected and it was now getting near to dinner time.

Finally he walked upstairs to change his clothes.

His valet had a bath waiting for him and Newman insisted on bringing him up a glass of champagne.

"You mustn't be late for dinner, my Lord. Cook's been working all day on your favourite sweetmeats. She were disappointed your Lordship was not there to enjoy the cake she'd made for tea."

"Tell her to put a piece of it by my bed tonight and then if I am hungry when I wake up, it will keep me going until the morning!"

Newman laughed.

"Your Lordship'll not be hungry if you eats all the dinner cook's got prepared. She's had the kitchen running about since we learnt your Lordship were arriving. If you stays for long my Lord, you'll be looking for new breeches because them you be wearing'll be too tight!"

It was the sort of thing Newman had said to him when he was a boy and the Marquis chuckled.

"I will be certain to see cook before I leave. I am definitely going tomorrow. I have already told the stables what time I want a horse and I shall be leaving soon after breakfast."

Newman looked at him in surprise.

"Your Lordship will be not going alone?"

"Yes, all alone, Newman, and I don't want a lot of questions asked as to where I am going and why. I am thus leaving you to keep those who are curious at bay."

"It'll not be that easy, my Lord. What'll I tell them when they ask where your Lordship has gone and when you'll be back?"

"I am sure you will think of something better than I could, Newman. The truth is I am disappearing for a while and it's no use anyone trying to be in touch with me."

"Well, it strikes me, that if your Lordship be up to mischief as you were when you was young, I'll do my best to keep them all from looking for you, but if they dies of curiosity, it'll not be my fault!"

The Marquis chuckled.

"You have always helped me, Newman, in all the strange things I do. I hope you will help me in this."

"I'll do my best, my Lord, but it's not a job I enjoy. Them women'll get real mad when they start to wonder where you've got to!"

The Marquis felt that Newman was really worried, but there was nothing he could do about it.

He walked slowly down to dinner and tried to make the conversation a little more interesting than it had been at luncheon – and only by talking instead of allowing his aunt to do so was it at all possible.

She kept on interrupting him by insisting that it was impossible for him to leave the next day, as there was so much she wanted to see on the estate.

After dinner they went into the blue drawing room where coffee and liqueurs were waiting for them and the Marquis had hardly had a sip of his before his aunt said,

"I am going to leave you two young people to get to know each other. I hope, Ivor, you will listen to what Edith has to say and I am sure you will find it interesting."

She did not wait for the Marquis to reply because she suspected he might protest and slipped out of the room closing the door firmly behind her.

He went to stand in front of the fireplace wondering what he should say and how he could avoid what he felt could be an uncomfortable *tête-á-tête*.

Then to his surprise Edith looked up at him and said in a small rather frightened voice,

"I am sorry! So very sorry!"

The Marquis looked down at her and thought if he was honest she was not completely unattractive – she was just young, unfledged and dull.

Then because of what she had said, he replied,

"I am afraid my aunt is very tactless and like all my family, she cannot help matchmaking without concerning herself with my feelings."

"You don't really want to – marry me?" she asked, stumbling over her words.

The Marquis shook his head.

"Quite frankly, no! I have no wish at the moment to marry anyone."

To his surprise she gave an obvious sigh of relief.

"I thought that was the truth, but I was still afraid."

"Afraid that *I* would want to marry *you*?"

"Yes!"

The monosyllable did surprise him, but at the same time he was interested.

"Then why did you let my aunt bring you here and make it so obvious as to what was expected."

"Lady Matilda is a great friend of my father and they arranged between them that I should meet you and that you would then find me a desirable wife."

The Marquis smiled.

"That sounds very unattractive. I suggest you tell your father I have no wish to marry anyone at present."

Then an idea occurred to him and he added,

"Is there someone else you would like to marry if you were not being pushed upon me?"

He saw a sudden light in Edith's eyes that had not been there before and he then suggested,

"I would like you to tell me the truth, because I feel now that you were not at all enjoying my aunt's blatent and rather clumsy effort at matchmaking."

"I was so very frightened! Terribly frightened, that you would say 'yes'."

"But why? Is there someone else?"

She nodded her head and then glanced towards the doors as if she was afraid that she might be overheard.

The Marquis sat down beside her on the sofa.

"Tell me about it, Edith, and perhaps I can help you in some way."

"It helps me so much that you do not want to marry me. I was desperately afraid when I came here that you would agree with Lady Matilda."

"I will never agree with her if I can possibly help it! Now tell me about yourself. I am really interested."

"You will not tell your aunt, my Lord?"

"No! Of course not, or anyone else."

"Then I want to marry someone who lives near us. At the moment it is too difficult for him to say anything to Papa because he knows that Papa would say that he has no house nor any money."

"Tell me about him," he asked sympathetically.

"I suppose I have loved him ever since we used to dance together at parties. He is four years older than me, and he says he has never found anyone he loves but me."

The way she spoke was very moving and there was a rapt expression on her face that seemed to transform her. From a plain and ordinary girl she became someone lovely but at that moment pathetic.

"What does your young man want to do?" he asked.

"He is keen on flowers. He saved up and worked his way to Nepal where they have such wonderful orchids and other strange blooms from the Himalayas."

The Marquis was surprised, but he did not interrupt.

"Peter brought back a great number of the most rare and unusual of these flowers. He claims that once he can grow them here in England, there will be a great number of people especially in London, who will want to buy them."

She drew in her breath before she added,

"They are very beautiful. Far more beautiful than any flowers on sale anywhere else."

The Marquis was suddenly interested.

"How does Peter know so much about flowers?"

"He has been interested in them ever since he was small. He used to bring me flowers from his garden when I was only a child. I knew then they were very precious."

"You say he has no house he can take you to if you marry him?"

"Peter said that he cannot approach Papa when he has nothing to offer except his love for me."

She spoke so simply that the Marquis felt touched.

"So what do you intend to do?" he asked.

"Papa did not make a fuss about me not wanting to go to London, as he is so much happier if he comes back home every weekend. Then Lady Matilda suggested that I should marry you and told Papa that I was wasting my time with Peter."

"So what has your father done?"

"He told me that if you asked me, I was to accept your proposal and I knew there was no point in telling him I loved Peter and that all I wanted was to be with him."

"I do understand what you are feeling, Edith, I have an idea which I think may help you and certainly save me from my aunt trying to force us down the aisle together."

"What is it, my Lord?"

"I learnt today that one of my cottages – in fact it is better than a cottage as it was used by my Head Gardener before he died – is empty. My manager suggested that as we do not require any more gardeners, we let it out and he is sure it could be let for quite a good sum if we allowed the garden and one or two fields to go with it."

Edith was listening wide-eyed as he continued,

"Suppose I invest in your friend Peter's idea of new flowers for London and for people like myself who love their gardens and want them to look different."

"Invest?" Edith queried.

"I was thinking perhaps I would not ask any rent from you, but I would fund what your fiancé would have to spend on starting up his business."

The Marquis paused for a moment to think.

"We would need to build special greenhouses, but when they are finished and all the flowers are ready, I am certain he would find it quite easy to sell them in London. He could then give me a small share in his profits."

Edith clasped her hands together.

"Do you really mean it, my Lord? Have you really a house where we could live?"

"You can look at it tomorrow, Edith, and I am sure your father would deem it is a very nice way for you to start your married life."

Edith gave a little murmur of delight.

"Of course your future husband, Peter, can pick the brains and use the experience of my gardeners. Several have been here for many years and I expect you know my gardens are famous for their beauty and originality."

"And Peter and I would really be a part of it?"

"That is what I suggest you tell Peter, and of course he will be able to explain to your father better than you can the possibilities of such a new business."

Edith gave a cry of sheer delight and then she flung both her arms round the Marquis who was sitting next to her and kissed his cheek.

"Thank you! Thank you!" she cried. "How can you be so marvellous? *So* different from what I expected?"

There were tears in her eyes.

The Marquis thought he had never seen a woman who had been so dull and dreary suddenly be transformed into anyone so radiant as if touched by a magic wand.

"Now what I will do, as I am leaving tomorrow, is to write all this out for you to take to Peter. Tomorrow before I leave I will tell my manager to help Peter in every way he can. You must look at the house and it can be done up by my own people to whatever you want."

"You are the most wonderful man in the world," Edith exclaimed. "I just cannot believe that this is really happening to me and I am not dreaming!"

"I am certain your father will see sense and realise that your happiness is more important than anything else, but I am afraid that *you* will have to deal with my aunt."

"I think I could deal with anyone now that you have been so kind to me, my Lord. It is all so fantastic. I wish I could run to Peter right away and tell him that you have solved all our problems."

"I only hope that is true. If you take my advice you will be firm with my aunt and not let her interfere. This will be your home and your happiness. The only person who should have a say in the matter is of course – Peter."

Edith laughed.

"Peter will feel that he can jump over the moon and like me that you are a kind archangel sent from Heaven."

"I will set the ball rolling for you. Now I suggest you go to bed and dream about Peter and no one else!"

"I shall dream we are thanking you and we will try to make you a huge fortune, my Lord."

She rose and when the Marquis had walked to the door to open it for her, he kissed her gently on her cheek.

"Good luck, Edith, and may all your dreams come true!"

"That is what you have done. Thank you! Thank you again!"

She looked up at him and added,

"I hope all *your* dreams will come true too. I shall pray they will."

The Marquis smiled.

"I doubt it. But your prayers may be more effective than mine!"

She smiled at him again and then she ran down the corridor towards the hall, almost, he thought, as if she was running back to the man she loved.

The Marquis walked to his desk.

He gave a little sigh as he pulled out a piece of paper to write down very clearly what he wanted for Edith and his manager was very able and would understand what he must do without making too much fuss about it.

At least, he mused when he had finished, there is one person going to bed really happy tonight.

'Now I can only hope,' he said to himself, 'that one day I shall feel as Edith is feeling now.'

He felt, however, it was most unlikely – unless an angel dropped down from Heaven, he was not likely to find the woman he was seeking.

It was with a feeling of satisfaction that he walked up to the Master bedroom.

After all, he had managed quite by chance to make one person happy.

If it had not been for the Duke's idea that he should seek love, he would never have changed Edith's life. It was with what he could only think of as a 'magic wand'.

'That is what I want myself,' he decided before he went to sleep.

Then he knew that he was asking the impossible.

He had so much already.

It was greedy to ask for more.

Then, as he closed his eyes to go to sleep, he had the intense feeling that in one room in the vast house Edith was praying for him.

CHAPTER FOUR

The Marquis set off at seven o'clock sharp before either of his guests were downstairs.

He was determined not to see his aunt again and he thought that she might try and spoil his plan for Edith if they talked about it.

He had not only written a letter to Peter about the house and his flowers but also to Lord Basildon.

He had told him how delightful it had been to meet his daughter and how interested he was in the flowers she had told him about and he was suggesting that he and Peter went into a joint partnership together.

He knew that Lord Basildon would find it difficult to refuse Edith the right to marry the man she loved.

Firefly was ready for him and his Head Groom had already fixed on the saddle two large bags that were similar to those used by messengers in the past.

They looked, the Marquis thought, rather strange, but it was the only way he could travel without a carriage.

If he had to be '*Mr. Nobody*' it was vital for him not to appear grand or proclaim affluence.

As he rode off from Milverton Hall he was thinking – as he had forgotten to do it before – what name he would now give himself.

He then decided that he could call himself Milton, as it was an ordinary name used by many and an easy name for him to remember.

He had been christened Ivor John, the latter name after one of his Godfathers and so he would therefore be 'John Milton' who was obviously of no social significance.

It was a beautiful day with just enough breeze and as he rode away he knew that the Head Groom and the two grooms were wondering where he was going.

They were obviously speculating as to why he was so mysterious about it.

It was, in fact, what he was wondering himself.

He rode through the nearby village where some of the blinds were still drawn and he thought as he did so that he was certainly a wanderer in a strange land with nowhere to go and no one to meet.

However, Firefly was enjoying himself and proving somewhat obstreperous.

The Marquis then left the main road and took to the fields – for the first two miles he was on his own land and when he reached his boundary, he took a road going North, having the idea that most of his friends would go South.

He passed through several small villages without seeing anything or anyone to attract his attention.

The hours passed by quickly and as he was feeling hungry, he stopped at a village that had a finer looking inn than the rest.

It was in black and white and faced the inevitable village green with a duck pond and it looked, the Marquis thought, as if he might get a decent meal there and he could make enquiries as to what was happening locally.

He rode Firefly into the back of the inn where he guessed the stables would be.

There was no ostler in sight and so he took Firefly inside the stable and found to his relief that it was clean. He located a bucket of water before venturing into the inn.

When he found someone in charge, he asked if he could have some food to eat.

"Would you like it outside or in, sir," the publican enquired.

"I think outside would be more enjoyable as it is a nice day."

He walked out onto the village green and sat down on the hard bench and thought that the village below him with its thatched cottages looked particularly attractive.

The publican hurried out to tell him that his wife would cook for him and to ask what he wished to drink.

"It's ain't often we 'as a visitor for lunch, sir," he said. "Everyone 'ere be workin' till the evenin'. Me wife complains that the food she 'as in store be wasted."

"Well, as I am hungry, she will not waste anything today," the Marquis told him. "Tell me about your village. I have not seen it before and so I know nothing about it."

"It be called Little Meadowick, sir, and as you can see, it's a right quiet place with nothin' much 'appenin'."

"What about the young people. Surely they find it rather dull here?"

"Well, some of 'em be tryin' to cheer the place up, sir, and if they don't do much mischief, I've nothin' to say against 'em."

"Tell me about those who are cheering it up."

The publican laughed.

"They be two young monkeys. Their father be the new Vicar and a very nice man 'e seems to be."

"So the Vicar's family are livening the place up? And how are they doing that?"

The publican laughed again.

"I thinks they'd better tell you all that themselves.

They be comin' in in a short while to buy what they wants for their parties they 'as in the woods."

"Parties in the woods! That does sound unusual."

"Tell 'em so and pr'aps they'll ask you to join 'em."

As the publican finished speaking there was a call from his wife and he hurried back for the Marquis's lunch.

It was plain, fresh and well cooked and he ate with relish and ordered a second glass of cider which he never drank in London, but it seemed appropriate in the country.

After he had finished the Marquis remarked,

"You are extremely lucky to have a wife who is such a good cook."

"She's as keen as I be to make a bit of money and move nearer to a town, sir. We want to 'ave more visitors 'ere and we be ambitious to make good money while we be still young enough to enjoy it."

As the man could not be more than thirty-five the Marquis chuckled.

"You have plenty of time ahead of you," he said, "but I do see that, as your wife is so talented in the kitchen, she must be rather wasted in the country."

"That be true enough, sir. Most people round 'ere wouldn't know a good meal if they ate it!"

The publican spoke scathingly and then before the Marquis could answer him, he saw two young girls coming across the village green and he guessed from the way they were well dressed that they were the Vicar's daughters.

He was not surprised when the publican came out with his second glass of cider and exclaimed,

"'Ere they be! Now you'll meet Miss Alice and Miss Melanie and make 'em tell you what they be up to."

The girls came nearer.

He thought they were about sixteen or seventeen and looked quite presentable but by no means beautiful.

As they reached him, they looked at him curiously.

The Marquis took off his hat.

"Good afternoon to you, ladies" he began. "I have just been hearing from the publican of this delightful inn how you are cheering up this village."

The elder of the two girls, who he thought must be Alice, responded,

"I expect he has been telling you stories about us. But as they are all half asleep here we have to pass the time somehow!"

"Do tell me what you are doing?"

The girls glanced at each other as if they thought he had some reason for questioning them.

Then as the publican came out with the extra glass of cider, he told them,

"This 'ere gentleman's been enjoyin' 'is meal while I've been a-tellin' 'im 'ow you young ladies be cheerin' up Little Meadowick and not afore it needs it."

"That is what we think," the girls chorused.

"Now suppose you sit down and tell me about it," the Marquis suggested, "and I am sure you will join me in a glass of cider or some other drink."

The girls looked at each other, before Alice said,

"That is very kind of you, sir, and we would like to accept your invitation, although I expect our father would say that we should not talk to strangers."

"As far as I can see there are not many other people to talk to and as I am alone, you will be doing a kind act in joining me."

Melanie laughed.

"That is what they always expect from the Vicarage and naturally it's the one place where kindness is free!"

The Marquis thought this was rather amusing.

"Now please tell me what you are doing."

"We are going to have a party tonight in the wood," Melanie answered. "If we had one in the Church Hall or anywhere else, there would be too many old people prying at us and saying that anything we did was wrong!"

The Marquis could well understand this.

"We therefore ask anyone who is young and wants to enjoy life," Melanie continued, "to join us in different places in the woods each time we have a party. The elders are not able to find us there!"

"That's a really good idea and one I would never have thought of myself."

The publican came out with a large cup of coffee.

"Me wife 'as told me that in the best 'ouses they always finishes a meal with coffee," he announced. "So I've brought you a cup, sir, which I 'opes you enjoys."

"I most certainly will and these two young ladies will be joining me in a drink. Perhaps you have something unusual for them."

"Now it just 'appens, sir, that the man who brings our stores yesterday 'ad some fresh lemons and me wife's made 'er lemonade that be very special."

"Oh, please let's have a glass," Melanie begged. "I love lemonade and they never have lemons in the shops."

The girls seated themselves opposite the Marquis.

"Where are you going?" Alice asked him.

"I am just riding about," he replied evasively.

"Then if you are stopping here you had better come to our party tonight," came in Melanie. "You are a bit old, but I think you would enjoy it!"

"I am sure I should and thank you very much. You have made a decision for me that I shall stay here tonight as the food is good and I'm sure the beds are comfortable."

Alice lowered her voice.

"He is a very nice man, but they are really too good for this village. We are always afraid they will leave."

The Marquis could understand this and he thought it was rather intelligent of the two girls to realise it too.

"Where do you come from?" he enquired.

"Our Papa was only a Curate at Bristol and when he was offered a Living here he thought he was going up in the world. He had no idea when he arrived how dull it is!"

"You had more fun in Bristol?"

"Of course we did," replied Alice. "We were going to a really lively school and at Christmas there were lots of parties. In the summer we could play tennis, swim and do all sorts of other things."

"I am really sorry for you, ladies, but surely you enjoy being in the country more than in the town."

Both girls wrinkled their noses.

"Not really!" said Melanie. "After all it is awfully dull having no one to talk to except the old people in the cottages. The young go out to work and Papa is, I think, already regretting he didn't stay on in Bristol."

"I am sure if your father agitated the Bishop who sent him here, he could find him a more agreeable Living."

"I doubt it," said Alice. "If you ask me, the Church puts a Parson wherever there is an empty Vicarage and no matter how good he is, they don't worry about him again."

The Marquis found this all rather interesting.

"I tell you what you could do to help us," Melanie proposed. "We have to carry the beer and food for tonight to the place we have chosen for our party."

She looked at the Marquis pleadingly.

"If you have a horse it would be much simpler if we took it on his back and we could go further than usual."

The Marquis smiled at her.

"I am quite prepared to help, madam, and I am sure your party is different to anything one would expect in this part of the world."

The two girls giggled.

"That is true enough," agreed Melanie. "But just you wait and see and you will be surprised how much our guests all enjoy themselves.

The Marquis was curious. It seemed strange that these two lively young girls should be living in such a quiet and peaceful village – yet unlike most girls he had met, they were willing to do something about it.

He finished his coffee and the two girls drank their lemonade.

Then he went to collect Firefly from the stable.

He took him into the yard just as the two girls were staggering out of the back of the inn with a number of beer bottles in a wicker basket.

The Marquis looked at it in surprise.

"We thought if we put the beer on his back," Alice explained, "it would be easier than carrying it in bags."

He felt doubtful and anyway he thought that Firefly had enough to carry. In addition he had no wish to discuss his well-packed clothes.

Nevertheless, if he was staying at the inn, it must be easier than carrying the heavy basket, but he did not want to overload Firefly as he might rear up and if he did, the beer would all fall to the ground and be smashed.

"I will tell you what we will do," he suggested. "I will talk to the publican and ask him if I can stay the night and then I can leave my luggage here and he can provide me with two bags to hang on either side of my horse."

The girls agreed with this idea.

The publican said that he was delighted to have the Marquis as a guest and the best room in the inn would be made ready for him.

He then took down his luggage and the publican's wife packed the bottles of beer in small sacks.

It all took time and the Marquis, although he had never done anything like this before, found he was more dextrous than the girls in making Firefly a useful carrier.

When the beer bottles were all arranged, there were also buns and biscuits to be taken with them and they too had to be placed in a secure position on Firefly.

Taking Firefly by the bridle he told the two girls to go ahead and show him the way.

They took him round the back of the inn and across a field that led to a large wood.

"We have not had a party on this side of the village before," Alice said, "and we never tell our guests where we are going until they meet us outside the churchyard."

The Marquis wanted to say he thought that it was an odd place to start the festivities, but they might not find such a remark as amusing as he did.

The girls went ahead to make sure there was no one watching and then they signalled for the Marquis to bring Firefly after them.

It was slow walking across the field. The Marquis wished he was riding, but Firefly did not seem to mind.

At the edge of the wood he realised that it was an excellently isolated spot to hold what he suspected would be a somewhat rowdy party.

There was a clearing which, he imagined, had been made long ago in the very centre of the wood and the girls decided that it was the perfect place for their party.

They told him that the last party had been down the other end of the village, and as it had been raining hard the mothers made a huge fuss when their children went home covered in mud.

The girls said they spent ages washing their dresses and much of the mud did not come off, while the Marquis did wonder vaguely why they should get so muddy, but he did not ask too many questions.

He was thinking that it was most interesting to meet people he would never have known before and to find that in their own way they were making the best of their lives.

Most of his richer friends moaned and complained loudly if they did not have exactly what they wanted at the moment they wanted it.

He and the two girls then unpacked the beer and the food, covering it up so that the rabbits would not be able to get at it.

By the time they finished it was getting late in the afternoon.

"You had better have dinner before you join us," suggested Alice, "and don't bring your horse or everyone will want to ride it!"

It was a point that had been troubling the Marquis as he had no wish for anyone to ride Firefly but himself.

"I will leave my horse at the inn and I will come at whatever time you tell me."

The two girls consulted each other and decided that by nine o'clock the party would be in full swing.

The Marquis had no idea what he would find there or exactly what they were planning and he decided that it would rather spoil things if he was curious, so he told them that he would be with them soon after nine o'clock.

He then went for a short ride on Firefly.

He found that the village was larger than he thought when he had first inspected it. The cottages were all small and rather poor. The Church being Norman was large and impressive and the Vicarage beside it was quite a pleasant looking house.

He felt most Parsons and doubtless the girls' father enjoyed being in the country as it would be easier for them and less demanding than being in a town like Bristol.

However he could very easily understand that the two girls, who were reasonably attractive, found it boring. Naturally they would miss going to parties and all the other entertainments easily available in a City.

The publican was delighted that the Marquis should stay for dinner and his wife excelled herself in providing good well-cooked fresh food.

He was, as it happened, not alone as several men came in. First they had their evening drink, sitting outside and smoking their pipes while they drank.

The Marquis talked to them and found they were all engaged in working on the land that he gathered belonged to several different owners – none of them seemed to be a Squire or of any particular Social significance.

Then as he was finishing his dinner two men, who were obviously commercial travellers, came in and sat at another table in the same room.

They were definitely having a poor reception from the villagers for their goods and they complained bitterly that this part of the country was so difficult and the sooner they were out of it the better.

The Marquis did not speak, but he listened to their conversation and found that the men were contemptuous of those who worked on the land, and they were even more convinced that it was a waste of time trying to sell their goods to country people – they had little or no money and were quite content with what they had already.

Listening, the Marquis thought this was something new as he had never worried if the people who lived in the villages he owned were happy with their lot or not.

His mother had been marvellous. If they were ill, she sent them fruit and honey and she always knew when they gave birth to a baby and his father had been concerned personally with the men who worked for him.

The Marquis knew now that if he settled down and lived at Milverton Hall, he would ensure that there were new ideas and new interests in his villages.

Of course, he thought, the young people were bored if they had nothing to do and like the two girls they missed the attractions and excitements of a town.

'It is something I must see to in the future,' he told himself.

At the same time he realised that he had been bored with too much entertainment in London, while the men of his age working for him had never had the chance of any entertainments – nor did they have the chance of learning about anything except their work after leaving school.

He wondered if other landowners had faced this problem on their estates and he decided when he returned to London he would discuss it with his friends at White's.

He finished his dinner and a glass of port that was not particularly good and he then realised it was time for him to go to the girls' party.

He walked out of the back of the inn and started to find his way across the field.

When he reached the wood the moon was coming out in the sky and the stars were already shining brightly which made it easy for him to see between the trees.

There was no question of there being any difficulty in finding the party. As soon as he entered the wood he heard the brash thump of music.

The man playing on the guitar was quite young and had obviously learnt to play well, but he was determined to make as much noise as possible.

The youngsters present, and there were the Marquis reckoned nearly twenty of them, were dancing, but it was in a way that would surprise anyone at a London ball.

The girls were dancing alone flinging themselves around and showing a good amount of their legs and the sight would undoubtedly have shocked his Aunt Matilda.

The men were doing very much the same, except that their idea of dancing was to jump up and down with their hands above their heads.

Alice saw the Marquis first and ran to him crying,

"So you have come! Now you will see what a good party we manage to have here where no one can see us and no one in the village can interfere."

She had to speak out loudly above the noise of the guitar and the shouts of the dancers.

The Marquis sat down on one of the fallen trees and watched them and he quickly realised that a large amount of beer had already been consumed.

The empty bottles had been kicked to one side in the undergrowth as the dancing continued with the noise of the dancers growing louder every moment and it continued until the music ceased and there was a roar of applause.

"More! More!" the dancers were crying wildly.

It seemed as if the younger they were the noisier they managed to be and they were all, the Marquis thought, working class and some of them were good-looking at the age of eighteen or nineteen and extremely athletic.

As if to demonstrate one of the men turned a quick somersault and two or three of the others tried to imitate him and there were shrieks of laughter from the girls. They had loosened their hair and lifted up their dresses to dance.

Another man started to play a violin and as he did so they twirled around and around mostly alone or holding hands with their partner.

They showed so much leg that the Marquis could well understand why they did not wish their parents to see them.

Melanie pressed a bottle of beer into his hand.

"You had better drink this whilst you can, sir. The dancing gives our guests a terrible thirst."

The Marquis smiled at her.

"Are you enjoying your party?" he asked her.

"It's a bit different to what we would be doing if we were in Bristol," she replied. "At the same time it cheers up the place and those who are dancing are willing to pay a shilling every time they come to a party like this."

"Is that what you charge them?"

"We made it sixpence to start with, but they drank so much we ran out of money!"

The Marquis was not surprised and she went on,

"Now we charge a shilling, but there are some bad debts and we don't have the heart, Alice and I, to tell them to stay away until they can afford it."

"That is indeed kind of you and I think it is very entertaining of you two girls to have thought out something as unusual as this."

He thought as he spoke that he would not want it to happen on his own land, but it was quite obvious that the young people in the villages must be amused and he only hoped that this enterprise on the part of the girls would not end in disaster.

He thought this again an hour later as two of the girls and the men they had been dancing with so vigorously disappeared into the darkness of the wood.

Nobody appeared to worry as to what they might be doing and the Marquis thought it would be easy for all the laughter to turn into tears, especially as there was no one to chaperone the younger girls.

The beer was by now finished and both the violinist and the guitarist were clearly exhausted.

"You play extremely well," the Marquis praised the violinist. "Who taught you?"

"My grandfather used to play and he left me the violin when he died so I taught myself, sir."

"Have you ever thought of going on the stage?"

The man shook his head.

"I've never been to a theatre, although I've heard about them. But I don't suppose anythin' I can do will be good enough for them."

He spoke quite simply without any regrets and the Marquis wondered if he should try to help him.

"What work do you do here in Little Meadowick?"

"I work on a farm. I look after the chickens and the lambs and help with the harvest."

"Do you enjoy it?"

"It ain't too bad and these girls from the Vicarage have made it amusin' for us as it's never been before."

"Do you like coming here and playing for them?"

"It's much better than playin' alone to myself and it wouldn't be so good without my friend on the guitar."

The Marquis felt that this must be the truth and the two girls had been lucky to find such talent in the village and then he found himself wondering if there was the same amount of talent unnoticed and unpraised in the villages round Milverton Hall.

Two more girls and men disappeared into the wood and Alice came up to him to say,

"We are going home! Have you enjoyed yourself?"

"Enormously!" the Marquis replied, "and I have been most interested. I think it is very enterprising of you and your sister to bring such enjoyment to the village."

Alice smiled but before she could say anything, he went on,

"I am sure that you should organise a concert in the village itself sooner or later and let them hear the two men who play your music. They undoubtedly deserve a larger and more attentive audience."

"It's something we have not thought about, sir, but it's certainly an idea."

She thought for a moment and then added,

"You do see that we should have to pay for the hall and I expect no one would want to spend money on seats."

"I am sure they would all come at least once."

"They might do if they never come again! But, as this only just pays for itself, we have to be careful not to do too much too quickly that we cannot afford."

"You are very sensible and I do hope you will find sooner or later two young men to take you to a proper ball. There must be one taking place somewhere in this district."

"I hope you are right, sir. In the meantime it is fun and we have had more customers, as you might say, at the last two parties than we have ever had before."

Alice spoke proudly.

"Now we must go home," Melanie said briskly as she threw three empty bottles into the thick undergrowth.

As she spoke one of the older girls and the man she had been with came out of the darkness of the wood and there was an air about them that told the Marquis all too clearly that they had been making love.

And he wondered if there was any reason why they should not do so or whether it would become a scandal in the village, and then the parties thought out so ingeniously by the two girls would come to an abrupt end.

He walked back with them over the fields with the moon shining brightly to show them the way.

"What do the parents of these young people think of this new idea of yours?" he asked keeping his voice low.

Melanie gave a little giggle.

"As they are not admitted, they have no idea what happens. We have told the boys and girls to say nothing otherwise we will certainly be stopped."

The Marquis was afraid that was the truth and he was sure the older people would be shocked at the way the young people danced together.

And if it was known what happened in the darkness of the wood there would certainly be an uproar especially among those who were more religious.

"If you ask me, you will have to be very careful not to get a bad name for yourselves and for Little Meadowick. I still think a concert would be a good idea. I am sure you and your sister have lots of talent if you want to show it."

"I can sing quite well," boasted Alice, "but I don't suppose anyone would listen to me at this party."

Her sister giggled and added,

"As you saw I can dance very well, but it might be called too fast for a Vicar's daughter."

"I would think, as you were dancing just now, that you could dance on the stage gracefully and elegantly. I would enjoy watching you at Drury Lane."

Both girls gave a little cry of excitement.

"Oh, you've been to Drury Lane! We read about it in the newspapers. But Papa could never afford for us to visit London, so I am sure we'll never see it."

The Marquis hesitated a moment and then he asked,

"Is there anyone in London you can stay with?"

"Oh, yes!" answered Alice. "We have an aunt who lives in Chelsea. But why do you ask?"

"Because you have been so kind to me tonight and amused me when I expected a dull evening by myself, I am going to leave you a little money before I leave tomorrow."

He smiled at them before continuing,

"If nothing else, it will take you to London for you both to watch the dancing at Drury Lane."

The girls stopped still in the field to stare at him.

"Do you really mean that?" they asked together.

"Yes, I mean it and what is more, I will give you the name of a box you can watch the show from, because it belongs to a friend of mine."

Melanie gave a little cry.

"It's really the most wonderful idea I've ever heard. Thank you! Thank you, sir! But you will *not* forget?"

"I promise you I will not forget. In fact when I get back to the inn I will write it all down for you carefully and you can call for it tomorrow afternoon when I have gone. But there is one thing I want you to promise me."

"What is that?" both girls chorused.

"That you will not tell anyone that I have sent you to London. Nor will you mention the name of the owner of the box."

"We promise you! We promise you!"

"I want you to think when you watch the dancing, how you can dance yourself and how you could make it a special event for this village. I feel it would encourage more young people to come here and perhaps as well to the Church on Sundays."

"That would certainly please Papa," sighed Alice.

The Marquis decided that when he did return home, he would have a word with the Archbishop of Canterbury and ask him to provide a bigger and better Living for the Vicar of Little Meadowick.

If the girls had been in the City, this is where they would be the happiest and the country is for the country people who know no other life and are thus more or less content with what they have.

When they arrived at the village, the young people who had been following them came up to say goodnight.

"It's been a real fine party, Miss Alice," one of the men said, "and I 'opes we 'ave another one soon."

"You are dancing better than you have ever done before, Joe, and our gentleman guest here thinks we ought to have a concert at the Church Hall."

"If you thinks anybody'd pay to see me dance you got another think comin', but I likes your parties. They be real fun."

He walked off into the darkness and the others bade them goodnight.

The Marquis thought it was time he went to bed so he thanked the girls again and promised them he would not forget to arrange for them to go to Drury Lane.

He walked back to the inn to find the publican was waiting up for him while his wife had gone to bed.

"What were them all up to, sir" he asked. "You've been away long enough."

"I had a long way to walk," the Marquis answered. "But they enjoyed your beer very much and needless to say there was not a bottle unopened when the party finished!"

"Well, 'tis good for business, if nothin' else."

"I think it is good for the village. Idle hands for the young is always a mistake. These two young ladies have many new ideas and the brains to put them into operation. I would support them all you can.

"I have persuaded them, I think, to hold a concert in the Church Hall. If you will say that it's for the Church or something the village needs people will come. The young would be able to show off how well they dance and how well they sing."

The publican stared at him.

"You've got a good idea there, sir. It's one I've never thought of meself. If you asks me it'll bring people to the village and we needs that more than anythin' else."

"It's a very beautiful village with a fine inn. I shall certainly recommend it to anyone coming this way."

"That's real kind of you, sir, and I assures you that you'll always be welcome 'ere."

"I shall depart early tomorrow morning. I will leave with you a letter for my two hostesses tonight and I am sure you will see that they receive it."

"Of course I will, sir."

The Marquis went to the stable to have a last look at Firefly. He was lying down quietly and content on the fresh straw the Marquis had provided.

"We leave early tomorrow, old boy," he muttered "and perhaps we shall find another adventure at the next place. It may even be as amusing as this one has been!"

He sensed that Firefly was nodding his head as if he agreed with him.

Then he patted his nose and left the stable.

Before he fell asleep he was thinking that if he did not find his goal, he had certainly discovered new ideas.

There was no doubt that he had made three young women happier than they had been before he met them.

'If nothing else,' he reflected, 'that is three good marks to me!'

CHAPTER FIVE

The Marquis rose early, had an excellent breakfast and then bade farewell to the publican and his wife.

"I have enjoyed being with you and I shall hope to come again," he stated.

"We've liked havin' you ever so much," the wife said. "As I says to me 'usband, you be a real gentleman, that's what you be."

The Marquis smiled.

"That *is* a compliment I appreciate."

He tied his bags onto Firefly and then set off from the back of the inn.

There were fields that had not been cultivated and Firefly was able to gallop over them and he only calmed down after travelling for quite a long way.

Keeping to the fields the Marquis moved steadily North, thinking that it would be interesting to see a part of England he knew little about and few of his friends came from the Northern Counties.

It was a warm day and the sun was bright but it was not too hot to be uncomfortable.

He thought it would have been pleasant if there was someone he could talk to and discuss the events since he left Milverton Hall.

He had learnt quite a lot about people in whom he had never been previously interested.

Yet there had been no sign of the beautiful young woman he was really searching for.

'If I go home empty-handed,' he mused, 'I shall be back arguing with my relatives about marriage. I cannot face that sort of conversation again.'

However it was bound to happen, unless by some miracle he found the rainbow the Duke sincerely believed was waiting for him.

He was feeling hungry when finally he reached a small village rather like the one he had just left, but the inn was kept by an old man and thus there was no chance of a cooked luncheon.

The Marquis was therefore obliged to make a meal of a cheese sandwich that was only just edible, butter that was questionable and bread that was undoubtedly stale and he washed it all down with some quite decent cider and he was lucky to have a cup of coffee that was drinkable.

"What is the next village or town to this place?" he asked the ancient publican.

"There be a small town not too far away," the man answered, "and you'll find if you wants to stay the night, there be quite a decent 'otel there."

The Marquis thought this was a good idea and he rode on on an empty road finding it slightly boring.

It was nearly six o'clock when he saw the roofs and spire of a town ahead of him. It was, he thought, a typical town that no one would visit unless they were interested in something local that was either bred or manufactured there.

He was to find out later that he was right and the town specialised in saddling, but there were few shops and they did not contain anything particularly interesting.

When he came to the hotel he could see that it was a hard ugly looking building of four floors and there was some not very adequate stabling behind it.

He thought it was too late for him to go any further and so he rode into the stable yard and asked an ostler if it would be possible for him to stay the night and the man said that he would tell the hotel keeper.

The Marquis looked in at the stables and as he had expected they were not very comfortable and not as clean as they might be and when the ostler returned to say that the hotel keeper was waiting for him inside, he demanded fresh straw.

"You'll 'ave to pay for it!" the ostler said somewhat aggressively.

"I am perfectly prepared to do that, my man, and I also require a clean bucket and you must show me where there is fresh water."

"You might be a-talkin' about yourself instead of your 'orse," the ostler remarked caustically.

"Strange though it may seem to you, my horse is very precious to me and, as he has come a long way, I am determined he should be comfortable."

The Marquis had been wise enough to bring some good oats with him that Firefly had enjoyed last evening and he was glad he had done so as there was nothing for him here but some rather tired hay.

When he had finished and more or less forced the ostler to find what he required, he gave the man a good tip and his attitude changed at once.

"That be real kind of you, sir," he said as he slipped the coins into his pocket. "I'll keep an eye on the 'orse. If 'e wants anythin' more, I'll give it to 'im."

As the Marquis walked into the hotel he realised it was a commercial building, a place he had never visited or stayed in before.

The manager was a middle-aged man with a rather ugly face, an abrupt manner and not very welcoming.

"I gather you wants to stay the night, sir," he said and it was as if he was protesting rather than encouraging the proposal.

"I need a comfortable bed and a good dinner," the Marquis responded.

Unexpectedly the manager laughed.

"That be asking a lot in this place, but I'll tell the cook to look to her laurels and see if there be anythin' in the kitchen you can fancy."

"That is good of you and I would like to see your most comfortable room. I would be grateful if you would send me up some hot water to wash in or a bath, if such a thing is possible."

"A bath!" the manager exclaimed in astonishment. "Why should you be wantin' that?"

"I have been riding all day. I am hot and tired and a bath, cold or hot, would suit me well."

"Well, I don't know about that, sir, it's somethin' we never gets asked for here."

"I should have thought in such a new town as this that there must be people who like bathing themselves and feeling clean. Even though normally in the depths of the country nobody bothers."

"Well, all I can say is that we don't get asked very often for a bath. I believe there's one somewhere in the hotel, but I've only been here just four months."

The Marquis had a feeling he was longing to tell him where he had been before and why he had come to this particular town, but as he was tired he thought it would be a mistake to start a long conversation. If it was anything to judge by what had happened to him in the past, it would go on for an amazingly long time!

Finally the manager took the Marquis upstairs.

On the first floor there were several bedrooms all of which appeared to be unoccupied.

"These be our best rooms, sir, and you have to pay a good price for them."

"I am quite prepared to do so. Now show me the best one."

The best was not particularly prepossessing with an iron bedstead in the centre of the room and to his surprise the Marquis gathered it was intended for a married couple.

The bed itself seemed small and hard, but as far as he could see the sheets were clean, so he declared,

"Very well, I will take this. Let me have the warm water to wash with and the bath as soon as possible."

"It'll be cold and I shouldn't have thought you'd want to sit in cold water for long!"

The manager walked away and the Marquis could hear him talking to himself as he went downstairs – clearly amazed at such an unusual request.

To the Marquis's surprise, although it took time, a somewhat battered hip bath was eventually brought in and with it were two cans of cold water and one can of warm.

There was apparently some difficulty in finding a large bath towel, but anyway he tipped the servants who brought up the bath and the cans so they were all smiling when they left his room.

Although the hip bath was uncomfortable, it was a joy to be able to wash completely. He thought that if the weather was warmer, he would doubtless find a lake or a river where it was private enough for him to swim naked.

Finally he walked downstairs to dinner.

It was to find that there were several people eating in the dining room and the food as he expected was just about edible, but completely unimaginative.

There was soup with little taste to it and beef that was thick and tough and the vegetables had probably been around for several days.

He refused a stodgy and unappetising pudding and instead finished his meal with cheese.

There was no choice of wines and he had to content himself with a light beer brewed locally.

As he had no one to talk to while he was eating, he looked at the others in the dining room and wondered what their history was and if there was anything about them he would find interesting.

As the people he had met had been so original last night, he was disappointed this evening.

The men were obviously travellers in trade and the women were dull, middle-aged and sat silent while their menfolk talked.

Then as the meal ended the Marquis was surprised when a young girl came into the dining room.

After looking around she walked across to him.

She was about twenty-five.

She had obviously made the best of her looks that were not up to much and her hair was undoubtedly dyed.

Without asking his permission she sat down at the Marquis's table and began,

"I've come to talk to you, because my uncle, who runs this hotel told me you were different from the usual lot of travellers."

"As they don't seem a very exciting bunch," replied the Marquis, "I can only be grateful I am different."

She smiled at him.

"You're different all right and if you ask me, you're a gentleman and shouldn't be here with this lot!"

"I think perhaps you are being rather unkind to your uncle's guests. I am sure the men sitting at the other tables are all tradesmen and will sell the goods you make here in this town all over the country."

She laughed.

"They try, but if you ask me they don't know how to attract a buyer as they should do."

"And how would you attract them?" the Marquis asked her without thinking.

Then, as he saw the expression in the girl's eyes, he realised that it was a look he had often seen before but in very different circumstances.

The girl lent forward putting both her elbows on the table and resting her chin on her hands.

"Now tell me about yourself, sir. I've never met a man who didn't want to talk about himself."

"Perhaps I am an exception," replied the Marquis. "So I am much more interested in hearing about you and your uncle. Does he own the hotel and do you help him?"

"No, he's just paid to manage it and them as owns it are very tight-fisted, I can tell you!"

"And what do you do?"

She gave him a sideways glance before she replied,

"I'll give you three guesses!"

The Marquis thought this was dangerous ground so he responded,

"Tell me more about the town. What entertainments are there here for young women like yourself?"

She laughed again.

"How do you expect me to answer that? The one thing we get plenty of is men. There's no need for me to tell you they're all of one sort with only one idea in their heads and that's why I wanted to talk to *you*!"

"I suppose by the one idea in their heads you mean they are trying to make money?"

"Well, some of 'em have other ideas. What about you then, what are you after?"

"I am just exploring the countryside," the Marquis answered. "I have come North and this is the first town I have visited so far. I am sure I shall find it interesting."

"If you can find anything interesting in saddles and shoes, then all I'll say is, I thought when I sees you, you'd be different."

"I am sure," he said, "as every man wants bridles and saddles you must meet people from other parts of the country and not just those making them."

"Well, I just can't be bothered with that lot. What I likes is men like yourself who have other interests and of course want a bit of fun."

"And what enjoyment is available here?"

Even as he put the question he thought he had been rather stupid.

There was a short pause and then she moved a little closer towards him before she purred,

"What do you think? Me, of course!"

"I have had a long day and you will understand that I need to retire to bed early. What might be rather rude on my part is not asking if you would care for a drink. Is there anything you would fancy?"

"If you put it like that, I could do with a drop of brandy. The waiter knows the sort I like."

The Marquis put up his hand and then when the waiter came towards him, he ordered a brandy.

"What I usually has, Jack!" she called, "and make it strong or I'll throw it at you."

"Now don't you get rough, Miss Flo," the waiter countered. "You knows it makes the Master angry."

Flo laughed and as the man hurried away to fetch her brandy, the Marquis asked,

"Are you rough at times?"

"I got a bit rough the other night when one of the men who were out for a bit of fun dares me to dance on the table."

She giggled before she continued,

"Course I did what he asked and my uncle was very angry not 'cos I was dancing but 'cos the table gave way and he had to send for a carpenter the next day!"

The Marquis smiled before he commented,

"Everywhere I go people seem to want to dance. Surely there is a hall in a town as big as this, where you could dance properly to an orchestra?"

"What you mean is a ball and they has them every now and then, but they isn't any fun. Ever so stiff they be with the men all dressed up while us women be expected to wear gloves."

"I should have thought you would like that. After all the balls in London are smart and everyone enjoys them enormously."

Flo made a grimace.

"I find all that 'how-do-you-do' and 'talkie-talkie' very dull. I really likes a man that's a man and that's what I thinks you are."

Again she was looking at the Marquis in a way that he knew so well, but it was a very coarse and rough gesture compared to the usual way he received it.

The waiter returned with a glass of brandy and the Marquis asked for his bill.

"It'll be ready tomorrow mornin', sir, with the bill for stayin' the night."

"Will you keep this table for me for breakfast?" the Marquis asked. "I hope to be down at eight o'clock."

The waiter nodded and walked away.

"Shall we go and sit in one of the rooms?" Flo then asked, "where we'll be alone."

"It's nice of you to suggest it, Miss Flo, if I may, but as I have to leave so early and have had a long day, you will understand that I am sleepy and need to retire."

He expected her to look disappointed, but instead she wore a different look in her eyes that troubled him even more.

He rose from the table.

"It has been delightful meeting you, Miss Flo," he said, "and I am sorry I shall not see you dance tonight."

It was the only comment he could think of.

"Don't you be too sure about that," she mumbled, "but having been bought a brandy I don't want to waste it."

"No, of course not!"

The Marquis held out his hand.

"The best of luck in the future."

She took his proffered hand and he felt her fingers squeeze against his and then she murmured,

"Perhaps that's not so far away as you think – "

The Marquis did not reply and he walked out of the dining room and up the stairs. He was well aware, without looking back, that Flo's eyes were following him.

When he reached his room, he closed the door and looked for a key to turn in the lock – there no sign of a key anywhere.

He looked round his room.

It was sparsely furnished and besides a double bed there was a dressing table with a small looking glass on it and there were also four hard chairs and a washing table with two basins and china jugs that matched them.

Then he saw, which he had not noticed before, that there was a chest of drawers just by the door and it looked strong and firm – it had been made by a carpenter who was not sparing with his wood.

In fact it took all the Marquis's strength to push it from where it stood to just in front of the door.

The door was now securely blocked by the chest and then he undressed and climbed into bed.

He was more tired than he thought and he reckoned that even the hardness of the mattress would not prevent him from sleeping peacefully.

He had just closed his eyes when he heard someone turn the handle of the door and push against it.

It opened just a quarter of an inch and then striking the chest of drawers, it was impossible for it to move any further.

The door was pulled back and tried again, but with exactly the same result. Then, as if the person outside had acknowledged defeat the door was pushed angrily back and he heard footsteps walking away down the passage.

It was then that the Marquis fell fast asleep.

*

Only in the morning when he awoke with a start did he see the chest of drawers where he had put it last night.

He had spent a peaceful undisturbed night and he mused that another time he might not be so lucky.

He would be wise in future to have with him some kind of contraption which would enable him to lock a door without having a key. It was something he had not thought about before and he wondered if such a device had been invented and if not, why should he not invent it himself?

Then he chuckled at the idea. After all most men would be only too willing to welcome anyone who came to their room and many would never have the opportunity of saying 'no' even if they wished to do so.

The Marquis hurried down to breakfast.

The waiter, hoping for a good tip, was attentive the moment he entered the dining room.

He ate eggs and bacon and drank a cup of thick and dark tea, guessing it would be a treat to many in the town.

To his relief there was no sign of Flo, nor did she appear when he said goodbye to the manager and thanked him for a good night's rest.

"Where you be going now?" he asked the Marquis.

"I have no idea, but it is definitely North and I hope to find something of interest in the next place I stay."

"We ain't got much to interest you here, sir," said the manager. "It's just the thought of money that brings in the travellers but a growing number go off empty-handed."

"Why is that?" the Marquis enquired.

"If you asks me, it's because them as has something to sell don't change what they're making from one year to the next."

"I suppose that might be said of a great number of things."

"Aye, sir, but one only gets something new when you've got too old to be useful any more. What is needed is products to brighten the eye and make you put your hand in your pocket. That's what sellin' be all about."

"You are quite right. I am surprised that you don't manufacture something yourself that would be marketable and perhaps a great success over the whole country."

85

The manager put his head back and laughed.

"We all hope to do so and if you asks what I really wants is a hotel somewhere by the sea or in a town where there be smart people with money and people that thinks to themselves they must have what's new and what's best."

"That is true and I am sure it would be a good idea for you to move to one of the more popular towns with a greater population."

"That's just what I be planning, sir, and I'll tell you one thing. My niece nags me day and night to be on the move."

"I can understand her feeling that perhaps you are wasted here."

"Well, I wishes you'd say that to them as runs this hotel. They own hotels in Liverpool and Glasgow which'd be very much to my liking."

"I hope you get one. Anyway goodbye and thank you again."

He walked out into the yard carrying his bags to put them back on Firefly's saddle.

Only when he had groomed his horse, saddled and bridled him, did he go out into the yard where he tipped the ostler and mounted Firefly.

Then as he was just beginning to ride onto the road, he looked up at the hotel windows and at one of them Flo was hanging out and waving to him. Her hair was untidy and she looked somewhat slovenly in the sunshine.

Nevertheless he swept off his hat gracefully.

Flo waved until the Marquis had left the yard and was out of sight.

'That is the sort of thing I have come all this way to avoid', he thought. 'The sooner I return and tell the Duke this is all a load of nonsense the better.'

Because he felt he had wasted a day and a night he hurried along the main road and it led him out of the town and back into the countryside.

It was with a sense of relief that the Marquis found himself once again in open fields, birds were singing in the trees and butterflies were fluttering over wild flowers.

Firefly was feeling fresh so the Marquis galloped him for some distance before pulling in the reins.

"You had better take it easy, Firefly," he muttered. "We have a long way to go. If nothing of interest happens in the next two or three days, I think we will go home and admit defeat."

Firefly did not answer, but the Marquis considered he was making the right decision.

He felt as if these last few days had been almost like years passing over his head and they had actually left him with nothing.

He began to wonder why he had been such a fool as to accept the Duke's challenge – it was impossible to meet anybody beautiful and exceptional when he was just riding along empty country roads and anyway he was apparently in a part of the world where there was absolutely no sign of his Social equals.

He had expected if he was travelling in the country to see extensive estates like his own or else to pass antique houses which had been occupied by Ducal or aristocratic families for centuries.

And somehow he would then be able to introduce himself and even though he was in disguise he would be accepted and not turned away from the door.

'I must be raving mad to believe that anything like that would happen and the Duke is as stupid as I am,' he blustered to himself.

So far he had been interested in the people he had met, but they had been the same sort he could have found on his own estate.

He wondered if he was being missed in London.

He was sure the number of invitations Mr. Harrison was dealing with had grown bigger and bigger day by day, and he had only to think about the comfort of his house in Berkeley Square and at Milverton Hall to know that most of his friends would think he was crazy.

Now here he was wandering about the country by himself staying in cheap and uncomfortable hotels like the one last night.

He had slept, of course he had slept, but there had been no valet to put out his clothes in the morning and no grooms to bring Firefly to the door.

As far as he was concerned this discomfort and list of irrelevant acquaintances could well continue for the next three months.

'The whole thing is ridiculous,' he reflected. 'The sooner I go back to reality the better.'

As he rode on he kept asking himself how he had been such a fool as to have accepted the Duke's challenge.

He had thought he would find it amusing.

"I am bored! Bored stiff!" he cried aloud. "You know as well as I do, Firefly, that the people we have met are not our sort and we cannot expect to be interested in them for more than three days at the most – if that!"

Firefly merely tossed his head and the Marquis felt that he was saying he found it uncomfortable too – he had been pushed into a small and sparse stall with none of his contemporaries to talk to!

"I will tell you what we'll do, Firefly," the Marquis said, as they rode on, "we'll give tonight one more chance.

Then we'll be brave enough to admit defeat and go home. As long as we do not have Aunt Matilda to make a choice of my future wife, I daresay one of those pushed on me by the rest of the family might be acceptable."

Firefly broke into a quick trot, showing in his own way he wanted to hurry home.

The Marquis wondered again if he was missing any amusing and exciting events in London.

The beauties of the *Beau Monde* were surely more alluring than Flo and he laughed as he thought that she had really tried to join him in his room at that hotel – she had expected that he would accept her blandishments as he had accepted those extended by the Countess.

Then he told himself that he was wasting his time, his youth and the joy and excitement that London gave him in its own way.

If he went back there, he would not risk seeing Juno again and yet as he knew only too well there were a dozen beauties to rival her – they would all hold out their arms eagerly if he so much as paid them a compliment.

"*We will go home*, Firefly," he cried aloud. "As far as I am concerned the sooner the better!"

He stopped for luncheon at the inevitable village inn where the food was scarcely edible.

The publican was surly and had no wish to talk to anyone except his wife and there were only two men eating there and one look at them told the Marquis they were dull and of no consequence.

As he rode on he resisted an impulse to turn back for home immediately, telling himself he would give the next village one last chance.

If it failed, then he would turn round and reach the Hall as quickly as possible and he would tell the Duke he had given up the challenge.

Then he would look intently at the girls the family would provide for him and he knew he had only to lift his little finger and they would come panting to the Hall or if he preferred it to Berkeley Square.

He had a feeling the proposed wives would all look very much like each other and there would be no particular excitement or adventure about any of them.

Nevertheless he would then have to marry one and at least he would do his duty to his title and his family.

And that would end the reproaches that had bored him for too long.

He rode on a little quicker as he realised that time was passing and if he arrived at a village and it was late there might not be a welcoming inn where he could stay.

He felt that Firefly was tired and he was tired too, but his tiredness was not only physical but mental.

'I was absolutely crazy to have come here in the first place,' he muttered to himself.

It was a joy a little further on to see the spire of a Church in the distance.

"It is our last port of call, Firefly," he announced. "I will make sure you are comfortable tonight, even if, like me, you find it lonely."

As he spoke he thought he could see the Countess's beautiful eyes looking up at him pleadingly and there were the soft hands and the eager lips of others he had loved.

'I must have been totally mad to come here,' he told himself again.

The village was only a little way ahead.

As he was about to quicken Firefly's pace, a man came out of the trees ahead of him.

He put up his hand.

He was fairly decently dressed and looked quite a presentable young fellow.

The Marquis drew in his reins thinking that perhaps he had lost his way and wanted to ask his assistance.

Instead the man called out to him,

"I can see you be a traveller, sir, and I wondered if you're a-comin' to the village ahead, you'd be kind enough to patronise a new inn my friends and I have just opened."

"A new inn?" the Marquis exclaimed.

"We bought up the old inn and then made it much more comfortable from the only other accommodation in the village."

"What is its name?" the Marquis enquired.

"*Waterfold*," the man replied, "and I can assure you we'd make you ever so comfortable at our inn."

"That is very kind of you," the Marquis said. "Of course I should be interested to see how you have done it."

"It's been so much hard work, sir, but we makes our customers really comfortable and one of us happens to be a good cook."

The Marquis smiled.

"Now that really interests me. I had a particularly nasty luncheon and am actually very hungry."

"I promise you won't be disappointed, sir, and the quickest way to where our inn is, is through this wood and over the field, otherwise you has to go the long way round by the road."

"Lead the way!"

The young man went ahead.

The Marquis saw there were thick trees on one side of him and there was a mossy path running straight through them and into a field on the other side.

As the trees came to an end the Marquis saw ahead there was a field with a gate opening into another field.

He drew Firefly to a standstill and they stood in the shadow of the trees while the man tried to open the gate.

The Marquis heard him exclaim,

"What the devil's happened here?"

Although he could not see clearly, the Marquis was aware that the gate had been tied up and he thought with some amusement that the farmer had found people using this route to the inn and had decided they should not use his land.

The man had drawn a knife from his pocket and was cutting through the rope.

Then the Marquis heard a little whisper beside him.

Looking down he saw to his astonishment that there was a young girl close by Firefly and looking up at him.

Before he could speak she said in a voice he could only just hear,

"Do *not* go with this man. He is going to steal your horse. I swear to you he is dangerous!"

The Marquis looked at her in surprise and when he would have spoken, she put a finger to her lips and added,

"Go straight down the road you were on before and past the Church. There are two large gates on the right hand side. Come there and I'll tell you what is going on."

She spoke breathlessly.

Then, as the Marquis was wondering what to reply, she turned and ran through the trees disappearing between the bushes that hid her completely from view.

He wondered if what he had heard was real or part of his imagination and he was also sure that he heard a horse riding onto the road he had just left.

Then as he turned his head back he saw that the young man in the field had cut the rope with his knife and was pushing the gate open.

On an impulse because he was curious the Marquis turned round and rode Firefly back the way he had come.

He heard the man who had opened the gate shout after him, but he galloped off down the road.

He went in the direction of the Church, the spire of which he could see in the distance.

CHAPTER SIX

The Marquis passed the Church.

A short way further on there were, as the girl had directed, two large rather impressive looking gates.

He reached them and turned into the drive and was surprised to find her just inside mounted on a good-looking horse.

"*You came!*" she exclaimed.

The Marquis smiled.

"Just how could I resist such a strange puzzle? You must tell me what this is all about."

"Let's go to the house," she now suggested, "and perhaps it would be wise to put your horse in the stables."

"You told me that man was going to steal my horse and as I cannot quite understand what you are trying to tell me, perhaps I should stay with my stallion."

"That is very sensible of you," she said. "Just as it would be very foolish of you to let that man persuade you to accompany him to his new inn."

They were riding up the drive as she spoke and then the Marquis saw ahead of him a very attractive Elizabethan house and the sun was on its pale pink bricks and shining on its diamond paned windows.

"Is this your home?" he asked her.

"It belongs to my grandfather."

He pulled Firefly into the courtyard near the front door and then, as if for the first time, he took a look at the girl who was riding beside him.

She was certainly very pretty in a soft gentle way due to the fact, he reckoned, that she was so young.

Her skin was the English strawberries-and-cream of which so much was written and her face was heart-shaped.

"I will tell you what we will do," she said, as if she had been thinking it over, "as you are nervous of leaving your horse – and you are quite right to be so – we will let him and Silver Cloud free on the grass opposite us. They will come to no harm and you can keep your eye on your magnificent stallion which I can see is exceptional."

"You are quite right," replied the Marquis. "That is exactly what Firefly is and if anyone is thinking of stealing him I would fight very hard to keep him."

"Of course you would, sir, and it is something I am afraid you might still have to do."

She slipped down from her horse as she was talking and the Marquis also dismounted.

He tied the reins on Firefly's neck and noticed that the girl did the same with dexterity.

As the two horses trotted eagerly out onto the green grass, the girl indicated with her hand a wooden bench that was outside the front door.

The Marquis sat down on it, took off his hat and crossed his legs.

"Now tell me what all this is about," he quizzed.

The girl pulled off her riding cap and put it down on the ground beside her.

She had very fair hair which, when it caught the sunshine, looked as if it was part of the sun itself.

"That man you were talking to," she began, "is a horse thief and for the moment I don't know quite what we can do about it."

"I think you and everyone else in the village should do a great deal if he really does steal horses."

"I know," she sighed, "but he does it so cleverly."

"Suppose that we start at the very beginning. First of all please tell me who you are and why apparently you are warning passers-by like myself against horse thieves."

"I am Vita Shetland and this is my grandfather's house. His name is Sir Edward Shetland."

The Marquis thought that he had heard the name somewhere before, but he did not interrupt her.

"These three men have only just taken over an old dilapidated inn at the back of the village. They repaired it themselves and now they have started to steal outstanding horses from travellers in a most outrageous manner."

There was so much emotion in her voice that the Marquis paused before he asked quietly,

"How do they do it?"

"You can hear the story direct from a man who is staying here simply because I found him so desperate and crying because he had lost the horse he loved."

The Marquis thought this all sounded very strange as she went on,

"It is what I understand has happened to a number of passers-by since, but I dare not interfere."

"Why ever not?" the Marquis asked.

"Because they are really clever. It was only today when I was riding back to the village and saw your horse ahead that I realised how magnificent he was. I knew then I somehow had to save him."

"For which I am extremely grateful, Vita. Do you really think they would have taken Firefly from me?"

"I will tell you exactly what would have happened."

She paused for a moment and it was as if she found it hard to speak quietly and calmly on the subject.

"There is no hurry! Firefly is safe now!"

"I hope that's true!" Vita exclaimed.

He thought perhaps she was being rather theatrical, and therefore suggested,

"Do go on with your story. What would the man struggling to force the gate open have done, if you had not warned me to ride away?"

"I bound up the gate last night. I must have known instinctively or perhaps it was God who told me that a very special horse would be coming here today."

She was looking at Firefly and added,

"He is superb, the most beautiful horse I have ever seen."

"That is exactly what I felt when I bought him."

Vita was so entranced with Firefly that she just sat still looking at him until the Marquis urged her,

"Go on. Do tell me why you tied up the gates and prevented me from following this man to the inn."

"When you reached it, he would have given you, sooner or later, a drugged drink, which is what he gave the poor man in the house, who you will meet and who still cries when he talks about it."

"*A drugged drink*," the Marquis echoed, "and then what would have happened?"

"You would have stayed the night in the inn. When you woke up in the morning, feeling, I imagine, extremely ill, you would have paid your bill and your horse would have been led out of the stable already saddled for you."

The Marquis looked puzzled.

"*My horse*?" he questioned.

"That is what they would have told you. Of course it was not your horse, but some tumbled down animal they had picked up cheap. While they had spirited away your thoroughbred to sell it at the next sale for a high price."

"How could they possibly do that? I should have pointed out that the horse was not mine and demanded the one I had arrived on."

"There are three brothers who own the inn and they employ, I believe, three or four men who are as crooked as they are themselves.

"They would all swear it was the horse you arrived on and by the time you called in the Police, your own horse would be miles away."

The Marquis was shocked.

He could understand that the average traveller had little money and no influence, and it would be impossible for him to protest very effectively that his horse had been changed for another when there were so many witnesses to say the contrary.

It was certainly a clever trick!

Because he was silent, Vita was watching him and then she laughed.

"You do see, sir, that I have saved your horse for you. I only wish I could drive those wicked men out of the village and send them all to prison!"

"It should be done," agreed the Marquis, "although after all you have told me, I realise it's rather difficult. Do they stop travellers every day?"

"I think they do, but I did not want them to know I was watching them. I therefore ride very quickly past the trees where one of the men waits for a stranger to pass by."

"And they have not tried to take your horse, Vita?"

"They would not dare. Grandpapa is an important man in the village and owns most of the houses. It would be very stupid of them to offend him, even though he is so ill at present."

"I think I have heard of him and I seem to recall your name."

"I expect really you are thinking of my father. He is a diplomat and he is often in the newspapers."

The Marquis gave a little exclamation.

Now he remembered why the name was so familiar. He had indeed met Roland Shetland at Carlton House and the Prince Regent had been very complimentary about the success he had been in Greece.

"Papa was sent to Russia by the Prime Minister a month ago," Vita told him, "and I was very upset because he would not take me with him."

"Do you often travel with your father and were you with him in Greece?"

Vita smiled.

"I was and it was the most exciting of all his recent journeys."

The Marquis thought she looked too young to have travelled on very many of them.

As if she read his thoughts, she added,

"I know I look as though I have stepped out of the cradle, but actually I am very nearly twenty-one. Papa has promised to be home for my birthday and I am to have a ball in London."

"I am certain that, as your father is such a success internationally, the Prince Regent will give a party for you at Carlton House."

As he spoke he suddenly realised for the first time that he was speaking as the Marquis of Milverton and not as plain John Milton.

"I am delighted that you have heard of Papa," Vita said, "and now please tell me your name."

"My name is John – Milton. I have read about your father in the newspapers and I can understand that you are very proud of him."

"Of course I am, but it is very lonely here without him especially as Grandpapa is unwell. My aunt, who had promised to stay here with me, had to go unexpectedly to Cornwall because her son had broken his leg at school."

The Marquis was silent and then he remarked,

"I quite understand that it might be very dangerous for you when you are alone here with, as I understand it, only the servants to look after you, if you try and challenge the horse thieves."

"That is what Evans, our old butler, says and the man who is broken-hearted because his horse was stolen."

"And what is he going to do about it, Vita?"

He was thinking it strange that this girl had taken the man into the house merely because he was so unhappy.

Vita made a hopeless gesture with her hands.

"What can he do? He has got no money and he was just riding about the country hoping to find employment."

She sighed and continued,

"He is so upset about his horse, the only thing he possessed. I have not suggested that he should work in the garden or in the stables, but I am sure when he is feeling better, that is what he will be able to do."

"You obviously have a very kind heart."

"I would hope so. But now, having introduced ourselves, we should consult our Head Groom as to where we should hide Firefly."

"Hide? Do you think he is still in danger?"

"I don't want to frighten you, Mr. Milton, but all the staff here are very old and have been with Grandpapa for a long time. They look after him well, but frankly, I am terrified of those three men."

"Do you think they will know where I have gone?"

"I am afraid so. You followed me down the road and that man knew that I was out riding. I passed him this morning and realised he was up to mischief.

"I don't know if I am unnecessarily apprehensive. All the time I am nervous. Those men are doing so well with their thefts that I cannot believe they will let such a beautiful stallion as yours escape their clutches."

"Now you are really frightening *me*," the Marquis said. "Let's go and look at your stables and see when the horses are locked in if it affords enough protection."

"Yes, let's do that," agreed Vita.

She jumped up and whistled and immediately her horse, which was cropping the grass, picked up his head and trotted towards her.

The Marquis had to fetch Firefly and lead him off the grass and he then followed Vita round the back of the house to where the stables were situated. They were well built and he thought looked fairly substantial.

But when the Head Groom was sent for, he stared at Firefly and gave an exclamation,

"That be real fine 'orse, you 'ave there, sir!" he said to the Marquis. "I ain't never seen a better."

"Nor have I, as it so happens, and I am very proud of him."

Vita told the Head Groom a little breathlessly what had just occurred.

"There's no stoppin' them devils, Miss Vita. The only thing we can do is to 'ope sooner or later them Police catches up with 'em."

"Has anyone made a complaint to the Police?" the Marquis enquired.

"There be only one Policeman in the village," the Head Groom replied, "and 'e's too scared to take 'em on."

Vita looked at the Marquis.

"It's true! We have talked it over and I did speak to the Policeman about it. But you will understand that he is on his own and Police Headquarters are miles away."

The Marquis well knew that the Police Force in the country was very slack and it was only after strong protests in Parliament that anything had been done about it

"Where should we put this beautiful horse of Mr. Milton's?" Vita asked.

The Head Groom scratched his head.

"Short of stablin' 'im in the 'ouse, Miss Vita, there ain't be nowhere except the stables."

"In the house. I never thought of that before. But, of course, Firefly can go into the old pantry."

Vita smiled as she went on,

"We never use it, but if they were clever enough to look there, which I very much doubt, they would find it far harder to break into."

"You be right, Miss Vita," said the Head Groom, I'll get the boys to make the old pantry ready for 'im."

He shouted out and two young men came running from the stables.

The Marquis could see there were several carriage horses as well as three which he was sure pulled a phaeton like his own. It was obvious, he thought, that Sir Edward was well off and enjoyed the comfort of a large staff.

The old pantry was as big as any ordinary sitting room might be, but in somewhat of a state of disrepair and as Vita explained it had not been used for a long time.

By the time the boys had filled it with fresh straw and turned the sink into a manger it was really, thought the Marquis, a most impressive stall for Firefly.

One of the grooms was sent into the house with his bags containing his clothes and having seen that Firefly had plenty to eat and drink, the Marquis then patted him and followed Vita.

She did not take him in the back way but went to the front door. By now the sun was sinking rapidly and the shadows were increasing under the trees as Vita led the way into a large and pretty hall.

There was a staircase with exquisite carvings and a fine array of ancestral pertraits.

An old butler with white hair informed the Marquis that his bags were upstairs in his bedroom.

"If Mr. Milton is going to change," Vita suggested, "we had better make dinner a little later."

"I'd thought of that, Miss Vita," replied Evans. "Cook is arranging it for eight-thirty."

"I am very sorry to put you to all this trouble," the Marquis pointed out.

"It's no trouble. It's very exciting you are here. I am so delighted that you are not crying pathetically on the road because you had lost Firefly!"

"I would much more likely be fighting those men."

"Not if you had been doped the night before."

The Marquis thought that, like most women, she had to have the last word.

He laughed.

"All right. You win! Now you have saved me, I have every intention of enjoying myself."

"We shall do our best for you, Mr. Milton."

They were talking as they followed Evans rather slowly up the stairs. Then at the top he turned left while Vita went to the right.

"Don't hurry," she said. "There is plenty of time. I am going to tell Grandpapa what has happened."

He saw her go towards a room at the far end of the corridor which he guessed was the Master suite.

While Evans led him to what he recognised with a faint smile, as being the bedroom, which in large houses was always kept for bachelors.

It was most comfortable and beautifully furnished, but there was only a single bed and he noticed that his bags had already been unpacked by a footman.

"I thinks, sir, you'll be real comfortable here," said Evans.

"I am sure I shall and I am very grateful, as you can imagine, for not having my horse stolen from me."

"These thieves and robbers be really terrible, sir," Evans replied, "but it's not right that Miss Vita should be tackling them all alone. They be the sort which sticks at nothing and if anything happened to Miss Vita, I think it'd kill her father when he comes back from Russia."

"I will do everything I possibly can to stop them carrying on their disgraceful trade," the Marquis asserted.

He thought as he spoke that he would have to get in touch with the Lord Lieutenant as there was no doubt that he would be able to close the inn and if there was enough evidence, the thieves would be thrown into prison.

At the same time he would have to reveal who he really was and that would put an end to him taking part in the Duke's challenge.

'I must think it all over carefully,' he told himself.

He was delighted as he began to undress that a bath was brought into his room and then set down in front of the fireplace and it was a proper sized one.

It was quite different from the bath he had paid for the night before and there was a can of very hot water and a can of cold. A footman who had clearly been well-taught to be a valet was there to assist him.

Then he put on black trousers and a velvet smoking jacket – his own valet had thought it was good enough for the country and he felt that he looked reasonably smart.

He walked downstairs at ten minutes past eight to find his hostess looking exquisite in a blue evening gown that was very suitable and most decorative.

Evans handed him a glass of champagne and then left the room to see if dinner was ready.

It swept through the Marquis's mind that this was very different to all that had occurred last night.

He raised his glass, saying as he did so,

"Let us drink to our success in preventing the horse thieves from getting one more into their grubby hands."

"I will certainly drink to that," smiled Vita. "But it is not going to be an easy fight."

"I am aware of that, but I am worried because I can see you are alone here and if they really made themselves unpleasant, I doubt even with your servants, Vita, that you would be properly protected."

Vita glanced towards the door as if she did not wish to be overheard.

"I know they are old and Papa said when he left me that it was time Grandpapa had some younger men in the house. Even the footmen are over forty and two of them suffer from arthritis!"

The Marquis laughed because he could not help it.

"You certainly have the strangest background when you are so young and so pretty."

Vita's eyes twinkled.

"It is a long time since I had a compliment. But when I was in France with Papa they came thick and fast and I appreciated every one of them."

"So you have been to France with your father."

"He likes having me with him, because Mama died when I was only fifteen and at times he is very lonely."

"I can understand that, except as far as I can make out, he is always travelling."

"That has been absolutely thrilling. I adored being in Greece, I loved Paris and he has promised to take me to Spain when he returns."

"You must be sorry he did not take you to Russia,"

"I begged him and begged him! But he said that it was to be a quick visit, but a difficult one and quite frankly he did not trust the Russians."

The Marquis laughed.

"That was the best reason of all! Of course your father was right, Vita."

"Anyway, he should be back in a month's time and then I shall be with him in London."

He was about to say that they would undoubtedly meet there and then he remembered his disguise.

"What did your grandfather say about yet another attempt at horse stealing today?" he asked Vita.

"I wanted to tell him all about it, but he is not at all well tonight. In fact the nurse with him said I was not to disturb him. So I shall keep the story until tomorrow."

As she finished speaking Evans announced dinner and they went into the dining room. It was a warm room with low windows all with diamond panes looking out over the garden and the table was decorated with flowers.

The Marquis thought with a sense of relief that it was what he was used to and it was so different to what he had endured these last two days of travelling.

What he found so interesting was his conversation with Vita as they ate simple but well-cooked food.

She had not only travelled with her father to places that the Marquis had visited himself, but she had also read a great deal about them, in fact he was pleasantly surprised that a young girl should have acquired such knowledge of the history of the countries she had visited.

He had found in the past that women longed for Paris because of the fashionable clothes and the gaiety of the City itself, but they never troubled to read of its Kings and Queens or the battles that had been fought on its soil.

When they came to Greece he had visited Delos and many of the Greek islands and he was astonished that Vita should know so much about the Gods and Goddesses of Olympus and the influence they had had on civilisation.

"You must find it rather dull here," he remarked when dinner was over and Evans and his elderly footmen had withdrawn.

Vita smiled.

"I have horses to ride. Papa bought three excellent ones before he went abroad and told me to look after them until he returned. I will show them to you tomorrow."

"Does your father have a house in the country?"

"Not now. We had one, but after Mama died Papa could not bear to be alone there so he sold it. We have a comfortable house in London. But he did not want me to be there when he was away."

Considering how pretty she was the Marquis was not surprised.

"But you must find it very dull here?"

"I would if there was not an excellent library," Vita answered, "and I will show it to you. It is larger than most private libraries and my grandfather collected books all his life and Papa has added to it extensively."

"When your grandfather dies you will live here?"

"Yes indeed. I am quite certain Papa will wake up this neighbourhood and things will be very different with him around."

She paused and there was a sadness in her eyes.

"Grandpapa was so amusing and so clever until he grew ill and it was always a pleasure to be with him. Now I can appreciate that the locals only occasionally call to see how he is and have not yet realised I am here."

"But they would not expect you to be."

"Of course when my aunt was with me, we visited her friends and they visited us, but when she went off to Cornwall I could hardly write and say 'can I come to see you?' when I hardly knew them. So with the exception of the Vicar there is really no one to talk to."

"What a shame and I hope it will not last for long."

"No, of course not. Papa will be back and then I shall be in London!"

She looked at him and enquired,

"You haven't told me where you live, Mr. Milton."

"I live in Hertfordshire. I can assure you that it's a far less isolated County than this one."

"Things happen here, even though you don't expect it and we must pray that nothing unusual happens tonight."

"I will drink to that, Vita."

They were laughing as they walked to the drawing room and then the Marquis commented,

"After the excitement of today, I think we should retire early. Tomorrow I intend to see the Policeman and find out if he realises how dangerous these thieves are to innocent travellers."

"If you can do that, you will be more successful that I have been, Mr. Milton. I think perhaps we should both have a ride before breakfast?"

It was a question because she looked at him almost pleadingly and he knew that it was what she really wanted and as it so happened he would like to ride out too.

"Of course we will and I am sure that Silver Cloud and Firefly will want to compete with each other."

"There is a place where we can have a really long gallop as good as any Racecourse – "

"I shall look forward to it," replied the Marquis.

They left the room and found the night footman – one of the older of them – was already seated in his padded chair with his eyes half closed.

"Don't move, James," Vita said as they appeared. "We are going to bed and I hope you sleep well."

"I find this 'ere chair be as good as any bed, Miss Vita!" James answered.

"I am sure you do and have happy dreams."

Vita walked up the stairs beside the Marquis.

"Tomorrow," she told him, "you will have to meet Mr. Tom Brown. He is staying with the Head Groom, but

109

I am not certain that he will keep him for long because he is always crying and his wife says it depresses her."

"I am not surprised. Does he still believe he might get his horse back?"

"He wants to find out where it was sold, but it's not easy and we can hardly ask the thieves outright what they have done with it."

They moved to the top of the stairs and Vita said,

"Goodnight Mr. Milton. I very much hope you will be comfortable."

"I shall be more comfortable than I was last night and thank you for a most amusing and delightful dinner."

He smiled at her and thought that, as she waved her hand, she looked like a Princess from a fairy tale.

When he went to his room he found that everything had been laid ready for him exactly as if he was at home.

His brush and comb had been put on the dressing table and beside them was a small pistol which he realised his valet had put in the very bottom of one of the bags.

"Do you really think I shall need it?" he had asked when he was told it had been packed.

"You'll never know, my Lord, what you'll find in them outlandish places – you be a-going without me," his Valet had replied diffidently.

"That is true enough, Croft, but I shall be surprised if I use it, then as you say, it might come in useful."

"As you're going alone, you'll need something to protect your Lordship," his valet had added gloomily.

The Marquis was thinking now that maybe the man was right and that he would have been a fool if he had gone off alone into the country without any protection.

He looked to see if the bullets slipped in easily and that part of the pistol did not require oiling.

Suddenly his door was flung open.

And Vita burst in.

She was wearing a pretty light green negligee over her nightdress.

"*They are here!*" she cried. "I looked out of the window and I can see them! They are creeping round the stable. If they don't find your horse they may take mine!"

"Show me just how you managed to see them," the Marquis asked her quickly.

Without commenting or arguing Vita started to run back along the corridor and the Marquis followed her.

At the far end near what he thought was the Master suite there was an open door and steps and he guessed it would lead up to the roof and he surmised that Vita must have slipped up the steps when she was ready to go to bed.

As he reached the roof he saw they had a clear view of the surroundings of the house including the greenhouses and the stables at the back of it.

Vita was now standing straight up against one of the high Elizabethan chimney stacks, which would prevent anyone noticing that there were two people on the roof.

As he joined her, she slipped her hand into his and whispered,

"Look over there! You can see that man clearly at the back of the stable."

She was right.

A man was edging nearer and nearer to the stable window, not exactly crawling but doubled up – it was as if by doing so he thought no one would see him.

Then as the Marquis watched he saw that there was another man just behind him while a third was coming in at a different angle.

They had in fact already reached the wall of the stable where it looked out on an open field and the Marquis knew if the men managed to break in they would find some way of taking the horses out.

It would be without anyone being aware of it and they would merely find empty stalls in the morning.

To his relief Firefly was not there, but Vita's horse was and several others he had noticed and they must be the thoroughbreds belonging to her father.

The two men had by now reached the stable and then as the third joined them, they started to prise open the stable window.

Even as they did so the Marquis lifted his pistol and he aimed it not at the men, but directly over their heads.

He pulled the trigger and the bullet flew out making a tremendous noise as it did so.

The Marquis fired three times.

Then the men were running back over the fields in a panic-stricken manner towards the road.

Only when they had disappeared out of sight, Vita, who was still holding on to the Marquis's free hand, said in little more than a whisper,

"That was *wonderful*! Wonderful of you!"

"It certainly scared them, but I deliberately did not hit them as I thought there would be an immediate Police enquiry. I want to make sure they are talking to the right people before they start a full investigation."

He was also thinking that if there was a wounded or dead man, he would then have to reveal who he was and it would be most embarrassing to have to explain why he was travelling in disguise.

Vita gave a deep sigh.

"How could you have had that pistol ready," she asked, "at exactly the right moment?"

"You must thank the person who packed my bag and Firefly for carrying it for me."

He very nearly uttered the word 'my valet', but just managed to prevent himself at the last moment.

"I don't think they will come back now," Vita said looking over the fields.

"I am quite sure they will not, tonight at any rate. So let's go back, Vita."

Immediately Vita turned towards the stairs that had brought them up to the top of the house and the Marquis followed her down and when they reached the corridor it was to find the night footman trembling.

"What's a-happening, miss?" he asked Vita.

"It's all right, James. There were some strange men at the stables, but Mr. Milton has frightened them away."

"I'm not surprised, miss. A bit of fire always puts the wind up 'em!"

The Marquis smiled.

"That is true enough!"

Vita was just opening the door to the Master suite.

"I must see if Grandpapa was woken by the noise."

She left the door wide open as she went in and the Marquis thought he should wait until she returned just in case she needed any further help.

She had mentioned that her grandfather had two nurses with him and he supposed one was with him now.

James was now going back down the front stairs to his comfortable padded chair.

The Marquis then slipped the pistol into the pocket of his evening coat, thinking what a good thing he had it with him and felt sure the thieves would not return tonight.

He then saw Vita come out of the bedroom door of the Master suite and he was just about to say goodnight to her when he realised that she was looking very pale.

Something must be wrong.

"What is it?" he asked her. "What is the matter?"

"I-I think" she mumbled, "Grandpapa – is dead."

"Dead!" the Marquis exclaimed and he walked past her into the Master suite.

There was a lamp burning by the bedside that was obviously kept alight all night.

In the huge four-poster bed with its traditional red velvet curtains there was Vita's grandfather – Sir Edward Shetland.

He had been clearly, when young, a good looking man and even in old age he still had his classical features.

He was lying on his back and his eyes were closed, but he was so still and that told the Marquis that Vita was right.

Very gently he stretched out his hand and touched Sir Edward's forehead and found it was cold.

Vita had not followed him into the room and when he went outside into the corridor he saw she had aroused one of the nurses from the next room.

It was very typical, the Marquis thought, that while James downstairs in the hall had heard the shots, the nurse had obviously only just woken up.

She hurried past him into the room and the Marquis saw her touch Sir Edward's forehead and his hand, as he had done.

Then she pulled the bedsheet over his face and he realised that Vita's grandfather really was dead.

The Marquis then went out to the landing and Vita merely looked up at him without speaking.

"You were indeed correct," he told her as gently as he could, "your grandfather has passed away. I don't think the shots from the pistol would have worried him, because he looks so peaceful and not in the least agitated."

"I – thought that too," murmured Vita.

"Would you like to go downstairs or back to your bedroom?" the Marquis asked her.

She drew in her breath and replied hesitantly,

"I don't want – to be alone – for the moment."

"Of course not. We will go downstairs and I will see if I can find you something to drink."

"I would – just like to talk to you – for a little."

"Of course and that is why I waited here for you,"

They went downstairs side by side and he took her into the room where they had been sitting after dinner.

"I know this may seem strange," said the Marquis, "but I see there is a bottle of champagne here. I am going to give us both a drink because I think we really need it."

Vita did not reply immediately and a moment or so later she muttered,

"I don't think Grandpapa minded dying. He had been in pain for some time and he now looks so at peace."

"I thought the same," the Marquis agreed.

He was standing by the grog-tray in the corner of the room and opened the bottle of champagne. He poured half a glass for Vita and half a glass for himself and then carried them back to where she was still sitting on the sofa.

She took a glass from him and then she stated,

"I don't want to be a nuisance to you in any way, Mr. Milton, but I am not certain what I should do now."

"Just leave everything to me," he replied. "I have dealt with both my father's funeral and quite a number of my relations. Just stay in bed. Tell yourself you have to recover from the shock and I promise you everything shall be done exactly as it ought to be."

"You are so kind. I am so very very lucky that I was brave enough to follow you into that wood."

"Why should you have been reticent?"

"I thought perhaps you would just laugh at me and think I was being tiresome and making a mountain out of a molehill."

"It certainly was not that! But what you will have to do tomorrow is write down the names and addresses of your relations. I have, of course, heard of your father, but you must have a great number of others."

He was thinking of how many he had himself and he was therefore surprised when Vita told him,

"There are not really that many. Papa was an only child and although Grandpapa had three sisters, only one of them is alive."

"The one in Cornwall?"

"Yes, that's right. She was the youngest and that is why her son who broke his leg is, I think, only seventeen."

"Seeing your grandfather was a Squire and you are a most respected family, the people who live near here will all expect to come to his funeral."

Vita gave a sigh.

"You must tell me what I must do and what I must say. It may seem rather strange, but I have only been to one funeral and that was Mama's which was abroad."

"In which country?" the Marquis enquired.

"Actually it was in Italy where she picked up some horrible germ that came from Africa and the doctors could find no cure for it. Papa was frantic and I felt I had to look after him.

"But it was a very small funeral," Vita added, "as Papa felt there was no point in bringing her home as the British Embassy had suggested."

The Marquis thought it was very sensible. He had always believed that it was a ridiculous waste of time and money when people carted dead bodies about, just because they wanted to be buried in some particular spot.

Equally he recognised that this had been a terrible shock for Vita.

There was no one but him to look after her.

'I really do find odd things to do,' he thought to himself and he felt compelled to do everything he could think of to guide the beautiful Vita over the shock of her grandfather's death.

They talked on a variety of subjects.

Then the Marquis took Vita upstairs and told her she must try and go to sleep.

"Don't think about what has happened or what is going to happen," he advised her. "Think about something pleasant – a book you have read, a place you have enjoyed or a person you are fond of."

She gave a rather tearful laugh.

"You do say such unexpected things," she smiled. "I cannot imagine anyone else telling me to do that."

"I have now told you what to do. Thus go to bed while I pull your curtains which I see you had drawn back before you went upstairs and onto the roof."

"I was just looking out to check that everything was safe. Then I remembered I could go up onto the roof and see far better – and it was a good thing I did."

"A very good thing. Now you have to go to sleep. Otherwise you know you will feel ghastly in the morning. Whatever else happens we are going to ride tomorrow."

"It is only due to you that our horses are still here."

The Marquis pulled the curtains over the windows and when he turned back he saw that Vita was in bed.

She was looking so glorious with all her fair hair cascading over her shoulders almost to her waist.

He stood by the bedstead looking down at her.

"Now you must close your eyes, Vita, and then start thinking about that delightful person you like, even if he is Apollo – and you are not to think of anyone else."

Vita gave a little laugh.

"You are making it into a game," she asserted. "So I will think about Apollo and *you*."

CHAPTER SEVEN

The Marquis made himself extremely busy.

He thought with amusement that he had never been so active before in his life.

First of all he visited the Vicar and agreed with him that, as it was going to be impossible for many relations to attend the funeral, the sooner they held it the better.

"I always think," the Vicar observed sensibly, "that if people are dead it is a mistake to have them in the house for very long."

"I do agree with you, Vicar," replied the Marquis. "Therefore I would be extremely grateful if you could bury Sir Edward Shetland as soon as possible."

The funeral would take place in two days time.

"If it is unlikely," the Vicar added, "that many of Sir Edward's relatives will be here, the locals will want to come for certain."

The Marquis was sure of that because he learnt that Sir Edward had been an excellent neighbour, just as he was good to the workers on his estate.

They were all upset by his death and the Marquis realised that the whole village would be in attendance on the day.

Fortunately the Church was only a short way from the house and the churchyard was actually on Sir Edward's land and the family tomb bordered on the drive, which the

Marquis thought was a relief. It meant there was no need to provide carriages for the household and Vita.

After seeing the Vicar he had gone at once to the Lord Lieutenant. He was an elderly man who had been a friend of Sir Edward for many years and was upset by the news of his death.

"Of course I will attend the funeral," he said, "and I am sure you can expect many people from the County."

"I would be grateful if you would give me a list of those who should be invited," the Marquis asked him, "as I obviously do not know them myself."

He had agreed with Vita that it would be a mistake to pretend he was not staying in the house or that they had only known each other for a day and a half.

"What we must say is that I am an old friend of your father's," the Marquis said, "and as I was travelling in this direction I called to see him – and that will also be an explanation for the Chief Constable of the County when I tell him about the horse thieves."

"It will be a good time to do it. I am sure everyone on the estate will go to the funeral, so the horses must be locked in very securely."

"I hardly think that they will come again after last night," the Marquis mused. "I frightened them away and I cannot believe they will dare to come near you again."

"I hope not," Vita sighed in a rather small voice.

He sensed that she was still frightened and it would be wrong to talk about it as it might make her feel worse, and so he suggested,

"We must be sure that there are plenty of flowers at your grandfather's funeral."

They went together to see the Head Gardener and he promised that the little Church would be filled with the colour and fragrence of endless blooms.

Instinctively they went from the garden towards the stables and the Marquis met Tom Brown about whom he had heard so much.

As he had no wife or children the Marquis could understand why he had given his whole heart to his horse.

Vita was patting all the horses and giving special attention to her favourite, Silver Cloud.

The Marquis inspected the stables and found they were strongly built and after scaring away the thieves, he felt it would be safe to put Firefly in with the other horses.

Then he told himself he was safe in the house and it would be a mistake to move him, but he appreciated that the ventilation was far better in the stables than in the old pantry. He was also suspicious that the pantry floor, which was made of bricks, was damp.

When they went outside the stables, Vita said,

"The grooms have told me they all want to come to the funeral. I think that the horses should be safe here at that time of day."

"I am sure they will be, Vita," agreed the Marquis. "I would suggest that we ride them early in the morning so that they have plenty of exercise and then put Firefly next to Silver Cloud."

Vita thought that this was a good idea and then the Marquis went to check that all the letters he had written to the locals had been delivered. The grooms had been riding from house to house with them and a number of people had sent back a letter to Vita with their condolences.

"I do wish we could get in touch with Papa," Vita sighed later in the day.

"I have already sent a letter to the British Embassy and one to the Secretary of State for Foreign Affairs," the Marquis told her.

"That was clever of you, Mr. Milton. I should have forgotten them."

"I have just thought as your father now inherits the Baronetcy it would be polite to notify the House of Lords."

He remembered that when his own father died they had said a special prayer for him in the House of Lords and stood silent for two minutes.

He had been careful not to sign his real name on any of the letters – he had merely inferred that he was a secretary working on behalf of the family.

*

It was on the afternoon before the funeral that the Marquis rode over to meet the Chief Constable and found, as he had expected, a rather bossy middle-aged man who was very conscious of his own importance.

When told him he was working on behalf of Miss Vita Shetland, the granddaughter of Sir Edward Shetland, he was impressed and became more polite.

"I will be attending the funeral," he asserted. "Sir Edward will be sadly missed in the County."

"I am very anxious," the Marquis told him, "that you should do so. Also bring with you several Policemen."

The Chief Constable looked a bit surprised and the Marquis related to him all that had been happening in the village and the saga of the horse thieves.

"As far as I can make out there are quite a number of horses whose riders have been enticed into the old inn and left with a different horse to the one they arrived on."

The Chief Constable looked astonished.

"It is a new way of horse thieving to me," he said. "I cannot understand why I have not been informed of this situation before."

122

"I think if you require a truthful answer to that, the Policeman in the village is far too scared to interfere with an inn where at least six men are working on this particular crime and being very successful at it."

The Chief Constable promised to do everything in his power after the funeral and he would meet Tom Brown and any others who had suffered from the thieves.

When he left the Marquis felt he had impressed on the Chief Constable that something must be done.

He added as he was leaving,

"I know that Miss Vita's father will be very grateful to you when he returns from the mission he has been sent on by the Prime Minister."

When he told Vita about his conversation with the Chief Constable, she was delighted.

"It is ruining the village and frightening the people in it. Because they are so afraid of what might happen they will not talk about it to me except in whispers. It is wrong that they should be so afraid."

"Of course it is," the Marquis agreed, thinking to himself he would definitely make sure that things changed before he finally left.

*

On the morning of Sir Edward's funeral he and Vita both went riding at seven o'clock.

As they rode over the fields in bright sunshine, the Marquis realised that Vita was undoubtedly one of the best riders he had ever seen.

She was so natural and unconcerned with herself that she seemed part of her horse and because she always talked to Silver Cloud, he felt that the animal understood every word she said to him.

They galloped across the fields and then came back slowly through a large wood. The squirrels were peeping out amongst the branches and the rabbits scurried ahead of them as they rode through the trees.

"It's very beautiful here," the Marquis remarked.

Vita smiled at him.

"I have often thought that fairies and goblins live in this wood, but I have only had Silver Cloud to talk to about them. That is why it is such fun having you here."

The Marquis smiled at her.

She was looking very lovely this morning with her golden hair tied back as if she was still a schoolgirl and yet she looked as if she had just stepped out of a fairytale.

They rode until it was nine o'clock and then they returned to the house.

The grooms were waiting to rub down the horses and the Marquis put Firefly in the stall next Silver Cloud.

"Now before you come to the funeral," he said to the Head Groom, "see that every door is locked and every window closed. It will be a little hot for the horses, but it is only for a short time and you can open up the doors and windows as soon as the Service is over."

"We'll see to it, sir, I don't suppose the Service'll take that long."

When he reached the house, he found that the body of Sir Edward had already been laid in his coffin, which had been made with unusual speed in the village. He had not suggested that Vita accompany him when he visited the undertaker as he thought it would upset her.

And he told himself it did not matter what one was buried in – once it was down in the ground the coffin was never seen again.

However the Marquis chose the best for Sir Edward and he was certain that the new Baronet would approve.

Vita was, he considered, very brave and very unlike the average woman.

She did not talk about her grandfather's death nor did she cry on his shoulder. He was so used to any woman who even heard of a bereavement making it an excuse for him to put his arms round her.

He admired the way Vita received the condolences of those on the estate, doing so calmly and politely without going into detail of how deeply bereft she was.

The nurses on his instructions made everything as easy as possible.

"I don't want Miss Vita upset," he said. "The less people talk to her about her grandfather's death the better."

"That is what I've always thought myself, sir," one of the nurses piped up. "People get more said about them when they're dead than kindness and consideration when they're alive!"

"That is what I have found. In this case Miss Vita is very young and has already lost her mother. It would therefore be a mistake for her to be deeply distressed over her grandfather."

"If you asks me," the nurse then replied, "it were a merciful deliverance. His pain was gettin' worse and there were nothin' the doctors could do for him."

"I am afraid it's too often the case with old people. And what is more important than anything else is to leave behind a memory of happiness and light and not just pain and misery."

He walked away as he finished speaking and was not aware that one of the nurses whispered to the other,

"Now there's a real nice young gentleman and a real sensible one too, if you asks me."

The other nurse added,

"I only hopes he looks after Miss Vita when we've gone. But you never knows with that type of gentleman. He might be after somethin' more spicey than a girl who lives in the country!"

The night before the funeral Vita confided to the Marquis before they retired to bed,

"It's so marvellous for me that you are here. You do see that as none of my relatives have turned up and I doubt if we will see any of them at the funeral, I would have been all alone and very miserable."

"It is you who is clever in saving me from the horse thieves, Vita. If, as you predicted, they had taken Firefly with them, I would only have had my flat feet to walk on and no idea where I could turn to for help."

"It was just fate that I went out that morning early and rode Silver Cloud through the village instead of going straight into the fields."

"It is obvious my Guardian Angel was looking after me, Vita, and he told you when you were asleep there was work for you to do at that particular spot."

"I really believe you are right, because sometimes I feel something wrong is about to happen. That was why I went out very early and tied the rope on that gate."

"I have done the same for tomorrow, Vita."

"Done what?" enquired Vita.

"I have told the grooms to tie up every gate on this land so that if by any chance while the Service is taking place or tonight for that matter, those thieves try once again to steal the horses, they would have to stop at the end of each field and open the gate before going through."

"That was very clever of you, Mr. Milton. I did not think of that. Most of the gates on Grandpapa's land are big ones and I would doubt if even Firefly would be able to jump them."

"I have no intention of trying as there is nothing more dangerous for a horse and its rider than a jump that is too high and will not fall if a horse catches his foot in it."

"I have a feeling you are a very good jumper, Mr. Milton. I think we should erect some jumps in the paddock and see who is best, Firefly or Silver Cloud."

"I will not let you jump anything that is too high for you," the Marquis cautioned. "I would hate to see you with a broken leg or a fractured collarbone."

"I would hate it myself, but I am quite certain you would sail over untouched and I would be annoyed if I was unable to beat you!"

"We will organise a race, perhaps for the day after tomorrow. Of course as you are a woman, Vita, I will give you a good start!"

"Now that insults Silver Cloud," she protested. "I am certain as I ride lighter than you, if we start equally, I would have a chance of passing the winning post at least a nose ahead of you – or more!"

"It's a challenge," agreed the Marquis, "and I will take it up the day after tomorrow."

Even as he spoke he wondered if he would be able to stay any longer.

After all now her grandfather was dead, Vita was unchaperoned and her relatives, if any of them appeared, would be very surprised if she was alone in this large house with only him to look after her.

However as Vita did not raise the subject he did not say any more, so when they went up the stairs to bed, he merely said,

"Don't worry about tomorrow, Vita, remember you promised me to think happy thoughts – and Apollo."

"I have not forgotten, but actually I will dream of a way I can beat you on Silver Cloud. Then neither you nor Firefly will be able to look at us in a superior way!"

The Marquis chuckled.

Vita waved her hand instead of saying anymore and closed her bedroom door.

As he walked to his own room, he thought she was extremely sensible as well as being enchantingly lovely.

Most girls, he had discovered, worried about their appearance and did not bother if they were sensible or not, all they were concerned with were the compliments they would recieve for their beauty.

'She is very sweet and unspoilt,' he told himself as he went to his room.

He was wondering if after tomorrow's funeral he should mount Firefly and return to London. It was what he had intended to do before the lovely Vita had saved him from the horse thieves –

As he was tired he fell asleep quickly.

*

When the Marquis reached the Church, he thought it looked very different to most Churches holding a funeral.

The coffin had been placed in the centre of the nave and was completely covered with white and pink flowers. It was so pretty and there were copious arrangements on the altar and at every window and opening of every pew.

As he escorted Vita into the family pew, he knew she was delighted with everything he had arranged. She did not say a word, but the expression in her eyes told him how grateful she was.

The Marquis had not consulted her over the Service but had chosen two of his mother's favourite hymns.

The choir from the village were mostly young and as the hymns were happy ones, he thought they sounded rather like young angels singing in the sky.

At his request the Vicar had made the Service very short and when they finished singing '*Praise My Soul the King of Heaven*' the coffin was taken slowly towards the West door.

Vita, escorted by the Marquis, followed it and after them came the Lord Lieutenant who was followed in turn by the Chief Constable and the local Squires in their order of rank.

When the coffin reached the family tomb, the men were already there to lift it into the ground.

The Vicar began a short prayer.

As they started to lower the coffin there was a shrill shriek from Tom Brown, who was with the rest of the staff.

The sound he made caused everyone to look in his direction.

It was then the Marquis saw that two horses were galloping at great speed down the drive.

Even as he realised one of them was Firefly and the other Silver Cloud, Tom Brown ran out in front of them.

Without pausing the rider of Firefly galloped right at him and knocked him clean over.

The Marquis then drew his pistol from his pocket and fired it at him.

When he had been dressing for the funeral in his dark suit, he had, without thinking, slipped his pistol into his pocket.

He had thought it absolutely impossible during the short time they would be at the funeral for the thieves to enter the stables, but somehow they must have managed it.

And then they had found they could not ride them as they had intended over the fields without opening the gates, so they had taken the chance of riding straight down the drive.

If the congregation had been in the Church, no one inside would have noticed the horses galloping by.

Now as the rider on Firefly aimed again at Tom Brown and missed him, the Marquis shot him in the arm.

With a scream he fell off Firefly.

The other man riding Silver Cloud was a little way behind him and the Marquis shot him in the shoulder and as Silver Cloud reared he fell backwards onto the ground.

It was then that Vita and the Marquis both ran onto the drive towards their horses and the Head Groom and his boys followed them.

Vita grabbed Silver Cloud's bridle and although the horse was shaking she talked to him gently and by the time the grooms reached him he was still.

The Marquis encountered a little more trouble with Firefly. He was rearing and bucking obviously upset by the noise and commotion.

His rider had pulled him over backwards because he was holding tightly on to his bridle and it was only as the Marquis managed to bring Firefly to a standstill and stroked him that he became calmer.

As the Marquis looked round he saw that the Chief Constable and several Policemen were looking down at the two men he had shot with his pistol and they were both lying on the ground writhing in pain.

"Take them to the Police Station at once," the Chief Constable ordered, "then our own men and as many others as possible will arrest the whole gang at the inn. Put these two into locked cells," he added, "and then send for the doctor to attend to them."

The Policemen hurried off to obey his orders.

The Marquis then turned to one of the grooms and instructed him to walk Firefly slowly back to the stables.

"Talk to him and make a big fuss of him," he said. "He will soon recover from the shock of what happened."

The Head Groom was holding Silver Cloud and the Marquis saw the two nurses were attending to Tom Brown.

One of them looked up,

"He's just bruised, sir, and when he fell down his nose started to bleed, but I don't think he's too bad."

"Get him into bed as soon as you can and let the doctor have a look at him before he bothers about the two men I shot."

"It was very good shooting, Mr. Milton," a voice beside the Marquis asserted.

He turned round to see the Lord Lieutenant.

"They must have thought they could get away with it because we were too busy with the funeral to guard the horses," he explained.

"I now realise that and I will see that all the men involved in this horse thieving are imprisoned for years or else transported."

"I have already arranged, my Lord," said the Chief Constable who had come up at that moment, "that they will be charged with horse thieving and attempted murder. It is only by a miracle they didn't kill the poor man over there."

It was then the Marquis added quietly,

"I think we should finish the funeral of Sir Edward. Then if you will all come back to the house there are some refreshments waiting there for you."

"Which we will need," the Lord Lieutenant smiled.

He turned and walked back into the churchyard and the Marquis and Vita followed him.

She was very pale but quiet and composed and the Marquis admired her resilience even more.

Most women of his acquaintance would be either crying or clinging to him because they were so upset by all that had happened – instead Vita held her head high.

They walked back side by side to where the Vicar was waiting for them and the Service was then concluded.

Vita threw a small bunch of roses onto the coffin as it was lowered slowly into the ground.

Only when the final prayer had been read did the Marquis move her away and they walked back onto the drive before any of the people crowding round the coffin were able to speak to her.

They walked quickly and in silence.

Only as they had nearly reached the house did they turn to see the Chief Constable's carriage following them and two or three other carriages were behind him together with several people on foot.

"If you don't want to talk to them all," the Marquis whispered, "I suggest you go up to your own room."

"Will they think it very rude?" Vita queried.

"You have been so brave and behaved beautifully as I indeed expected you to do. There is no need for you to entertain these people, so I will do it for you."

He was certain they would only want to talk about the drama on the drive.

Vita gave him a little smile.

"Thank you very much, Mr. Milton. It was all very terrifying but now Silver Cloud and Firefly are safe, thank God."

"We will go and cheer them up afterwards. Now slip upstairs now and I will join you as soon as I can."

132

She gave another little smile and ran upstairs.

Evans had all the refreshments ready in the dining room. There was champagne for the men while there was coffee and non-alcoholic drinks for the women.

The Lord Lieutenant had a great deal to say about the events of the day.

"It is a disgrace to the village that this sort of thing should occur," he chuntered. "I cannot understand why the Police did not act sooner."

The Marquis could now hear the Chief Constable making eloquent excuses for the shortcomings of his men.

Upsetting and dramatic as it had been that day, it had brought home to the Lord Lieutenant and the Chief Constable that more Police were needed in small villages.

'We live and learn,' he told himself as he spoke to several of the women present.

When they all eventually left, it was with a sense of relief he could go upstairs to see Vita.

He knew he would find her in what had been her mother's boudoir that opened out of her bedroom.

The room was full of flowers and Vita was standing at the window with the sunshine turning her hair to gold.

As he walked in and closed the door behind him, she looked round and then she ran towards him.

"Have they gone?" she asked breathlessly.

"Yes, they have all gone and you were marvellous."

She looked up at him.

Without even thinking he put his arms round her and pulled her against him.

Then his lips found hers.

As he kissed her he knew it was entirely different to any kiss he had ever given or received in his whole life.

Her lips were very soft, gentle and unspoilt.

He kissed her for a long time before he raised his head and as he did so she said in a whisper he could hardly hear,

"I love you. How could you ever be so kind and so wonderful to me?"

"And I love you, Vita. I have never known anyone who could be so brave in such difficult circumstances."

Then he was kissing her again.

Kissing her as if he had been waiting for ever for the ecstasy that swept through him.

Now he had found it he could hardly believe it was true.

When at last Vita could speak she said,

"I suppose I ought to go and ask how Tom Brown is. If he had not screamed, we might not have noticed the thieves on our horses."

"I thought that too, my darling Vita. I asked Evans before I came to find you. He said that the nurses had put him to bed and he was very comfortable. He only had one painful bruise."

"Oh, I am so glad and we must find him a horse to replace the one he lost."

"Of course we must."

Then realising what he had said the Marquis added,

"*We* is exactly the right word, Vita. I want to ask you, my precious one, *if you will marry me.*"

He felt her move even closer to him.

"Are you sure you want me?" she whispered.

"I want you as I have never wanted anyone before. In fact I know now I have never really been in love until this very moment."

Then he was kissing her again and kissing her until they were both breathless.

With a little murmur Vita hid her face against his shoulder.

"You are so sublime and so perfect," he breathed. "I am finding it hard to believe you are real."

"And you are like Apollo himself and I knew when you told me to think about him that all I really wanted to do was dream about you instead because I loved you."

"You *knew* you loved me, Vita?"

"I could only think how terrible it would be when you left me," she murmured.

"That is something I would have no intention of ever doing," the Marquis declared firmly.

He kissed her again.

Then as the door opened behind them, the Marquis released her.

To his surprise a man was standing in the doorway.

As she looked at him, Vita gave a little cry.

"Papa!"

She moved from the arms of the Marquis and ran towards the man who had just entered and flung herself against him.

"Papa, you are here! When did you get back?"

"I came back and heard yesterday when I reached London that my father was dead. I tried to be here sooner, but I have learnt now from Evans that the funeral is over."

As he was speaking, he was looking at the Marquis.

Then he suddenly exclaimed,

"*Milverton*! What are you doing here?"

The Marquis smiled.

"I wondered if you would recognise me. We met, if you remember, Sir Roland, at Carlton House."

"Of course I remember, but I was told downstairs it was a 'Mr. Milton' who had arranged the funeral and who was looking after my daughter."

"It's a long story, which we will tell you later. But I am actually at this very moment asking your daughter to marry me."

For a brief second there was an expression of sheer astonishment on Roland Shetland's face and then he said,

"Of course I am delighted if you love each other."

Vita slipped her hand into the Marquis's.

"I do love him, Papa, and he has been so kind to me and coped with everything that has happened. Even those wicked and horrible horse thieves."

"That is exactly what Evans was telling me," Sir Roland replied, "but I was *not* expecting to find you in the arms of the Marquis."

"The Marquis!" Vita exclaimed. "Are you *really* a Marquis, Mr. Milton? And I suddenly realise I don't even know your Christian name."

"I am afraid I *am* a Marquis, Vita, and my name is Ivor and actually you have made me one thousand pounds for which I am most grateful."

"But how and – why? I don't – understand."

"I will tell you about it later, but, for the moment, we should greet your father who must have endured a long journey here."

"Long and extremely difficult," Sir Roland agreed. "Of course I would like to have been at my father's funeral but I must be content with your wedding whenever it takes place."

They walked downstairs to the drawing room.

Sir Roland was hungry after his travelling and so he ate paté sandwiches and drank a glass of champagne with relish.

It was then that the Marquis suggested,

"I have an idea that you may not approve of, but I would like it more than anything else in the world."

"What is that?" Sir Roland enquired.

"That Vita and I should be married *immediately*."

It was now Vita who was surprised, but she slipped her arm through the Marquis's and asked,

"Do you really mean, Ivor, that we don't have to wait the full six months of mourning?"

"I mean just that," asserted the Marquis. "If your father will permit it, we will be married tonight if possible – then disappear on a long honeymoon."

He paused for breath before he added,

"When we come back, we will have a big party for you to meet all my relatives and for me to meet yours at my house in London. In addition there is a certain Duke you must meet, but more about him later."

"I think it's a good idea," said Sir Roland, "to be married at once as it would be very frustrating to have to wait for six months. If you are married tonight secretly, no one will know what has happened until you are away from England and spending your honeymoon in some outlandish spot."

"Not particularly outlandish," the Marquis replied, "but we will certainly go to Greece and I have other ideas for the Mediterranean that I have always found delightful and which I am sure Vita will find entrancing."

"Anywhere with you," Vita whispered, "would be wonderful."

The Marquis looked down at her and for a moment as their eyes met, they both forgot her father was present.

Then the Marquis declared firmly,

"Yes, we will be married tonight. Then tomorrow we will leave immediately on my yacht."

"It sounds too marvellous," sighed Vita. "I adore the sea, but I would be happy anywhere as long as I was with you, Ivor."

"That is exactly what you will be, my darling."

Watching them Sir Roland thought he had never seen two people look so happy or so delighted with each other.

He was very well aware of the Marquis's positon in Society and he knew too he was exactly the sort of son-in-law he wanted for his daughter and they were obviously very much in love.

Because Vita was so intelligent and very different in many ways to other girls of her age, he was certain they would be exceedingly happy with each other.

"I will send for the Vicar and we will arrange your marriage immediately," he said. "What I know will please you is that I came down from London with a new team of horses and I have beaten every record."

Vita gave a cry of delight and her father went on,

"After you are married you must waste no time in leaving the country before anyone realises that someone as important as the Marquis of Milverton has been caught at last!"

The Marquis chuckled.

"That is the right word for it. There is only one person who you can tell after we are well away and out of reach of what has occurred."

He then told them about the challenge that the Duke had given him and his friends at White's, and how he had been on the verge of giving it up as an impossible dream as the search was becoming extremely mundane – that was until Vita had rescued him from the horse thieves and they fell so unexpectedly in love with each other.

"It is the most romantic story I have ever heard," Sir Roland exclaimed, "and one that will delight everyone when they hear it."

The Marquis held up his hand.

"Don't forget that will be in six months time and you must swear the Duke to secrecy too."

"I will do so," Sir Roland assured him. "But the one person who must be told is His Royal Highness. You know as well as I do he likes to be the first to know every secret. He will be extremely offended with both of us if he is not informed confidentially as to what has occurred."

"I have already thought of that. What you must tell him is that we were married the day before you arrived and not the day after. In other words we were married secretly because we did not want a grand wedding the day before your father passed away. We had intended to go off on our honeymoon as soon as you returned."

"That at least is the truth," affirmed Sir Roland. "I will make it clear to His Royal Highness that, as the rest of the family are being kept in ignorance and have been told you are merely visiting friends abroad, he will be the first to give a party for you when you return as man and wife."

The Marquis then threw back his head and laughed while Vita clapped her hands.

"It's more and more like a fairy story," she sighed. "But I am so happy to be the Fairy Queen."

"Of course you are, but only I will be aware of how perfect you are until we return to England."

They enjoyed a very amusing luncheon and then Sir Roland announced meaningfully that he was going down to inspect his father's grave and talk to the Vicar.

As Evans and the footmen had left the dining room, the Marquis said,

"If you arrange for our wedding to take place after dinner tonight no one will ever know either here or in the village that anything unusual has happened. We could then leave early tomorrow morning."

Sir Roland nodded.

"That is a good idea. I am going to stay here and take over my father's place and deal with any members of our family who will be sorry they were unable to attend the funeral. They will be only too ready to help me now that I am the 'King of the Castle', so to speak."

"I envy you your superb horses, Sir Roland, and I will entrust you with my precious Firefly who is, without exception, the best stallion I have ever owned."

"I will take very good care of him, Ivor. If he is at all homesick, I will send him back to Milverton Hall."

"I think he will be quite happy with you and thank Heaven it is safe here now those horse thieves have been imprisoned."

"We will be eternally grateful to you for facing up to them and not letting them get away with it."

Sir Roland had now heard the whole story and had found it almost unbelievable.

*

If the Marquis had arranged the funeral particularly well, Sir Roland was just as effective with the wedding.

Wearing her prettiest white dress and putting on a veil just before she reached the Church, Vita and her father walked together down the drive.

The stars were coming out in the sky and the moon was rising up above the trees. There was a silence and a strange quiet that comes out at night.

It made Vita feel as if she had stepped into another world and was no longer human but part of Heaven itself.

When they reached the Church, the flowers seemed even more beautiful than they had been earlier in the day for her grandfather's funeral.

Now there were six lighted candles on the altar and the moonlight shone through the stained glass windows.

It made those in the old Church feel as if the Spirit of God was with them and angels and archangels were singing overhead.

The Marquis was waiting for Vita in front of the altar.

Sir Roland gave her away and the Marquis placed his signet ring on her finger.

When they knelt to receive the Blessing, Vita was sure that they were not just four people in the Church, but they were surrounded by all those who had loved them.

She knew that her mother was near her and even her grandfather was smiling his approval of their marriage.

When they rose after the Blessing, the Marquis took Vita down the aisle on his arm and they stepped out into the night leaving Sir Roland in the Church with the Vicar.

They walked in silence between the old oak trees and as they neared the house Vita pulled off her veil.

In the moonlight it seemed to the Marquis that she wore a halo and it made her appear as Divine as the moon and stars themselves.

There was only one sleepy footman to let them into the hall and they walked upstairs without him paying any particular attention to them.

Only as they reached Vita's bedroom did he kiss his wife's forehead very gently.

Then he walked into his room.

In her bedroom Vita undressed, putting on a pretty nightgown and drew back the curtains so that moonlight swept into the room.

She climbed into her bed and waited with just one candle alight by the bed.

The Marquis came in and she drew in her breath.

As he stood looking down at her, she knew that this was the most perfect moment of her life.

The love in his eyes was the love she had always prayed she would find.

The Marquis was thinking the same.

It seemed incredible that at the end of his journey he had found the impossible.

Someone who was perfect in every way.

Someone who aroused in him feelings of ecstasy he had never known before.

For some moments he stood looking down at her and neither of them said anything but reached out to each other with their souls.

Even before he blew out the candle and climbed into the bed beside her, Vita knew that she was his.

As he then pulled her gently into his arms, she felt as if she was flying to the moon and reaching out to touch the stars.

It was a blessing they could never lose.

"I love you, my precious, my darling," the Marquis breathed passionately.

His voice was very deep and different.

"And I love you," Vita whispered. "I love you with all of me. When you told me to think of Apollo, the God of

Love, I could only think of you. But I was afraid you would never love me."

"I love you in a way that it is impossible to explain, Vita. I just know you are mine and we were created for each other when we were born. Nothing in the future will ever keep us apart."

"That is what I want you to say. Oh, darling Ivor, kiss me and teach me about love and make certain I will always do as you want."

"That is exactly what I am going to do. I know, my precious, that a vivid and exciting future lies ahead of us because we are together. We will explore the world and help everyone we meet to be as happy as we are."

Then he was kissing her.

Kissing her gently but demandingly.

Her kisses were the nectar of the Gods.

When he finally made Vita his, they passed through the Gates of Heaven and reached the Divine.

*

A long time later when the moonlight seemed to fill the whole room Vita whispered,

"I love you, my wonderful marvellous husband. I love you with all my heart and soul. There are not enough words to tell you how much."

"And I adore you and worship you, Vita. You are part of me. Nothing and no one can ever separate us."

They knew as they spoke that the moonlight was blessing them as well as Apollo.

God himself had brought them both together in the strangest way.

And God would never allow them to be parted.